13 SHORT STORIES

Cathy McGough

Stratford Living Publishing

WHAT READERS ARE SAYING...

DANDELION WINE

U.S.

"Dandelion Wine is a feel-good short story, although the epilogue made me feel a bit sad at how things change. It was kind of nice to briefly visit a time when things were different.

"A short, sweet story down memory lane to a simple life in an idyllic summer day."

THE BRIGHTEST STAR

"Love never fails. Linda and William's life of love is summed up in this short story. A story of frustration and struggle while holding onto love through it all."

MARGARET'S REVELATION

Canada

"I started reading this novella within minutes of buying it, and once I started, I had to finish. I really enjoyed this story. It's well written, and you couldn't help but feel for the protagonist. And the surprise at the end made my jaw drop."

DARRYL AND ME

U.S.

"Spooky. A short bittersweet story about a woman's tragedy and her attempt at coping while pregnant."

U.K.

"Great story. Excellent emotions. I really felt for Cath and Darryl."

THE UMBRELLA AND THE WIND

U.S.

"Sci-Fi at its most modern and timely. Short, good read."

"The author spins an imaginative Sci-fi story stirring up hazardous wind, a flying umbrella, spinning green bottle and more. A short story with fast action."

India

"What a thrilling ride! The flow is superfast and the writing consistent and smooth. Somehow, it reminded me of Jerome K Jerome and Three Men In A Boat."

U.K.

"The mother of bad weekends meets the alien. Written with a dry wit, this is a bizzarro tale featuring an alienesque massive green object, umbrellas, and guns. Highly imaginative if not bonkers story that will have you gripped to the last page. Full marks for creative imagination, Cathy McGough. May have you laughing aloud and spilling your coffee."

DEATH WISH

U.S.

"I read this in half an hour last night after I went to bed. I felt sad for this man who felt that his life was pointless. McGough leads the reader to the very edge, and even when he has gone beyond the point of no return, you have no idea how things will end. A great story to read at lunch or coffee break."

"I liked Cathy McGough's creativity in producing a short novella of 20 pages with a large life changing experience of one man who couldn't find his life purpose."

"I had this book in my Kindle for awhile, but when I finally decided to read it, I didn't put it down until I finished it.

Though a very short read, the plot and characters are fully developed. Loved it."

"It reads like an episode of Tales from the Crypt or Twilight Zone."

"I loved it and as I read, I was asking WHY? When I found out, I was horrified, that sort of thing is my worst nightmare."

U.S. AND U.K.

"The author skilfully uses the character's internal monologue to reveal his life and the decision he is grappling with. Gripped me right to the end. This deftly told tale is a very entertaining read and I highly recommend it."

Contents

Dedication

FOR DIANNE

Preface

Dear Readers,

This collection of Short Stories includes six of my readers' favourites, and seven new short stories which I wrote during the pandemic.

They say 'out with the old and in with the new' but I say let's look at the entire view.

Happy reading!

Cathy

DANDELION WINE

I T WAS 1967 AND summer was nearly over when I pulled my rickety red wagon along a pebbly dead-end road. The clatter of my carriage wheels was a familiar sound, to people along our route.

"Nice day for a stroll," I would say.

"It certainly is. Now you have a good day," they would reply.

If my friend Sandra and I were lucky they'd bring us some ice water, cola, or lemonade. Although we didn't live nearby, we were treated kindly by most. Most but not all the homeowners.

"Don't be a pest," Dad always told me, and I wasn't. I always minded my own business. I didn't dilly-dally or try to draw attention to myself. Could I help it if the squeaky wheels squeaked?

I was a girl with a purpose, so it didn't matter that my arms were aching even though I wished they'd grow faster. It didn't matter when the cart overturned in a pothole or when it rolled into the ditch.

Still, the crazy woman in one of the houses was on my mind. I dreaded walking by her house alone.

On other visits she yelled at us for doing nothing. Or swore at us. Once she even sent her dog out, drooling and barking. The mutt protected the road like it was a part of her property. I glanced up at the roof, where the old Canadian flag was blowing in the breeze. Some said she refused to fly the new flag with the big Maple Leaf. She and her dog gave me the heebie-jeebies.

My breath quickened as I approached the dreaded house. Since it was a dead-end street, I had no choice but to pass. I stopped and looked back to see if Sandra was coming. No sign of her yet.

Then I remembered Grandma's lucky rabbit foot was in my pocket. It gave me courage. I pulled the wagon along with both arms and hurried on by.

I knew Old Lady Macguire was there. I didn't have to see her. I could feel her. In the house on the left, behind the curtains. Giving me the evil eye. She hated kids, all kids.

A few houses later, I nearly tripped over my shoelace. I steadied the wagon before squatting to retie it. As I did, I glanced back over my shoulder and saw the curtains twitch. It didn't matter now. I was out of her evil eye reach.

"Hey wait up! Wait UP!" the sound of my friend's voice accompanied her sandals connecting with the stony road. Finally, my best friend made it. Sandra was always late for everything.

I turned in her direction and watched her run by Old Lady Macguire's place. She was out of breath when she reached me. We fell into each other's arms. We'd both made it safely past the old witch's abode.

"It's about time!" I said a bit impatiently as we broke apart.

"Sorry, had chores to do and mom was determined to brush out my hair. She said I was a public disgrace!"

"Your dress is pretty," I said taking note of the pleats and bows adorning the two front pockets. It was pretty, and completely inappropriate for picking fruit.

Sandra grabbed her half of the wagon handle with one hand and pressed down the front of the dress with the other. "I hate pink," she said.

Her hand next to mine fit perfectly and we were able to pull the cart along side by side with ease.

"Mom made me promise to stop at the corner store on the way home and buy a loaf of bread." She reached into her pocket, "See, she gave me twenty-four cents, plus a nickel so we could split a banana popsicle."

"Oh, that's something to look forward to." Banana was our favourite flavour.

We kept on walking. A dog barked somewhere behind us.

"To get the popsicle money, I *had* to wear this stupid dress."

"It's not stupid," I said lying and wishing I had a pretty dress of my own I could wear on a day that wasn't a church day. With two brothers, one sister and another baby on the way it wasn't likely I'd be getting a new dress anytime soon.

Sandra whispered, "Did you see her?" I knew she meant Old Lady Macguire. "Did you feel her evil eye on you today?"

"No, because I crossed my fingers and my eyes." I lied.

"Good thinking," she said shifting most of the weight onto her side and asking, "Want me to take over and pull for a while?"

"Nah, you might dirty up your dress." Sandra guffawed. "It's more fun together," I said as we strolled by Mr. Holiday's house and then on by Mr. and Mrs. Otter's house.

Nearly at our destination, we became quiet. As best friends we didn't have to be talking all the time. The purpose for our journey was a shared one dependent upon Miss Virginia Martin's *black currant bushes. If there were plenty of currants, she might let us take a share. If the pickings were scarce our trip again would have been for nothing.

"I can't wait to see how much fruit there is," I said.

"I have a feeling we'll be lucky," Sandra said.

We stopped and looked at Miss Virginia's house. The front garden was always immaculate; it was like the wind knew to keep blowing the trash and leaves away so they didn't mess up her pretty lawn.

Since I was a little girl, I always looked for friendly faces in houses. Mom said it was a habit I'd grow out of in time.

Miss Virginia's house had an unusual but kind face with two round windows at the top. When the blinds were pulled halfway or all the way down, they looked like eyelids. This feature was different than any other houses I'd seen.

Between the eyes, a nose grew. A nose made of bricks. The difference was, these bricks were standing up, whereas the rest of the bricks were sideways. It gave me chills as it was like the builder knew he was making a nose feature just for me. I know that probably sounds daft.

Then onto the mouth below, which was fashioned by the double doors. A stained-glass window across the top made it look like a row of teeth with braces.

I loved standing and looking at the house because it was also a place where nature thrived. I laughed remembering how the ivy growing wildly sometimes made it look like the house had a mustache or a beard.

I noticed Sandra was humming *Penny Lane*. She always hummed when she was bored. *The Beatles* were okay, but I preferred *The Stones*.

Sandra brushed the blond hair from her face, as the flies buzzed around her like her perspiration was an invitation to swarm.

I released my grip on the wagon and stood on my tiptoes to see over the fence. I hoped I was tall enough this time, but no such luck. Sandra gave it a go as she was a fraction taller, but she couldn't see over either. I held the wagon steady while Sandra got in and tried to see over but even that didn't do the trick.

"I think we better just go up there and ask," Sandra said.

"Fair enough."

We pulled the wagon onto Miss Virginia's front lawn and parked it, then strolled up the long driveway which was lined with flowers. Sunflowers nodded their heads, bowing to us like we were royalty passing among them. A few dandelions struggled in their cousin's shadow.

"Remember the time my dad let us taste the dandelion wine he made?"

"It was the awful-est thing I've ever tasted," Sandra said.

"I know, but you still shouldn't have spit it out." We laughed remembering the wine splattering all over Dad's shirt. "Dad thought you were very rude."

"I didn't mean to be." She glanced at her feet. "Hey, you know what? We could ask for sunflowers and sell them."

"They are pretty, but let's keep to the plan. Mrs. Smith said she'd pay us two quarters (fifty cents) for as many black currants as we can carry, so we already have a buyer. We don't know anyone who wants sunflowers."

"I just thought, someone might want the seeds. But okay."

I glanced at my friend and chose to say nothing more on the matter.

At the bottom of the stairs, we gathered our thoughts. From experience, we knew that it was not what we said, but how we said it that mattered.

Last time we failed, miserably. Miss Virginia said the black currants weren't ready yet. She said how excited she was to create some new recipes for The Annual Fall Fair.

Miss Virginia was famous in our County, having won numerous Gold Medals for black currant related recipes. She often had her picture in the local paper, sometimes even on the front cover.

So, keeping the fruit to herself was her right, but sharing was what the world was all about. We hoped to convince her to allocate a portion of black currants to us.

On that visit, disappointment must've shown on our faces, because Miss Virginia invited us to help her pick apples and pears instead. She offered to pay us ten cents each, but that wasn't enough for us to get what we wanted. We thanked her for her kind and generous offer but declined.

"What if she says no?" Sandra asked, wincing as she looked into my eyes.

I reached out and touched my friend's long blond locks, and then gave the strand a little pull. "Come on, let's find out."

Sandra started to run, but I caught her in time and mouthed the words "DECORUM," to which Sandra replied, "Huh?"

"Slow down," I whispered. "Remember we are young ladies."

We giggled. Sandra smoothed down the front of her dress again.

I took my hands out of my pockets and reached for the knocker. Before I even touched it, Miss Virginia threw the door open. She was smiling, not just with her mouth but with her eyes. She was happy to see us, that was a good sign.

"Who do we have here on this fine morning?" she asked, knowing full well who she had there because Sandra and I had been coming back all summer. We'd climbed up on her porch more than a dozen times asking after the black currants.

"It's us, me and Sandra," I said and the two of us kind of curtseyed. It was our best try at curtseying, although the real

Queen of England might not have thought so. Miss Virginia applauded.

"Well, well," Miss Virginia said, as she looked us up and down. Sandra in her pretty pink dress and me in my overalls. "Don't the two of you look…" She hesitated. "You girls remind me of…" She paused, her words and facial expression now frozen. Her eyes went sad, only for a second. She smiled. "You two look like a picture, in fact, I'd like to take a picture if you don't mind?"

Her change from happy to sad and back to happy again made my stomach-ache. I looked at Sandra and we agreed. Miss Virginia invited us inside to wait while she got the camera ready. In the other room we could hear her opening and closing drawers.

"I'm worried about the wagon," Sandra whispered.

I backed myself up and looked out the window. "Everything is fine." After that, I kept my eye on the wagon as I didn't want it to go missing again.

Like the time when we went inside for a glass of lemonade. When we came out again it was gone. We walked and walked trying to find it, but there was no sign of the wagon.

Sandra and I went home. I was terribly upset, crying like a baby. The wagon meant a lot to me, squeaky wheels, and all. It had been a Christmas present from my grandparents.

Our parents and friends searched until the streetlights came on. The next day we put an ad in the Lost and Found. It was found beyond the forested area, overturned in a farmer's field.

We, Sandra, and I knew who put it there. Of course, it was Old Lady Macguire, but we had no proof. Dad said you should never accuse anyone of anything without proof, but we'd seen her watching us with her evil eye.

Just then, Miss Virginia returned carrying a Kodak Instamatic. I'd seen an ad for it in Dad's copy of Life Magazine. The 104 was a real corker.

"Gather round now girls."

"Wouldn't the light be better outside?" I asked.

She smiled and opened the front door.

We waited on the porch, trying not to fidget too much while Miss Virginia decided where she wanted us to stand to get the best light.

I leaned on the porch wall, trying to get a glimpse of the black currant bushes but it was no good.

"Hmmm," Miss Virginia said, "why don't we go into the garden? With everything blooming we could take some wonderful photos."

Sandra and I grinned.

We made our way down the stairs. Sandra reached the bottom in one quick leap much to my disdain. Miss Virginia didn't seem to mind. We strolled along behind her, taking in every word. "This is where the parsley grows, and here are my tomatoes. My, how tall they have grown this year. Nothing like fresh tomato sauce. And over here is my dandelion patch. I use them to make dandelion wine."

Sandra gasped and made a face.

Miss Virginia didn't seem to notice. "And here is my black currant patch, but of course you girls already know that one."

I tried not to look too excited and threw a glance back over my shoulder at the wagon assessing how much we could carry in one trip. I wished I'd brought it into the garden with us.

I felt Sandra's arm brush against mine. I noticed her mouth was hanging wide open as she gazed at the currants. She looked like a dog waiting for his dinner.

"I'd close it young lady," Miss Virginia exclaimed, "Unless you want to catch some flies."

Sandra hid her mouth behind her hand.

Miss Virginia laughed in almost a giggle as we looked at the black currant bushes in full bloom. The fruit was hanging there, ready to be picked. Lots and lots of currants. We were so excited we let out a squeal.

"First the pictures," Miss Virginia reminded us. Miss Virginia tried to find the best angle possible considering the trees were stretching out in the sunlight, creating shadows.

I realized with so many currants ready to be picked, Miss Virginia would need our help, and she'd have to offer us more money than she did when she asked us to pick the apples and the pears. With apples and pears, we were limited to what we could reach. With the black currant bushes, we could walk around and pick every single currant.

"May we pick some now?" Sandra asked.

I shook my head hoping she hadn't blown our chances.

"I'd like a photo with the black currant bushes behind you. Careful now, don't squash them or knock off the fruit and don't for goodness sake, eat any before the photo or your hands and mouths will be stained. Oh, I just remembered. Now, you girls just wait here while I nip inside for a moment."

Alone, positioned smack dab in front of the currants, it was like they were calling our names. We fidgeted. Waited. Tried not to listen to the whispering black currant bushes. They invited us to pick one. To have a taste.

"This is crazy," Sandra said. She opened and closed her fists. Turned and faced the black currant bushes.

I turned too. "I agree. But if we wait for the black currants, we'll make enough money selling them in one afternoon."

"Right," Sandra said, as she eyed the fruit clusters. "But I need to have one."

"Don't," I said.

"But she'll never know!"

"Okay, let's pick one berry."

"But they're so small."

Sandra picked one and so did I.

I popped mine into my mouth, and the sweet and sourness made me want another. And another. We grabbed a handful and tossed them into our mouths. The currant juice blanketed my tongue.

Miss Virginia returned to the garden.

We must've looked quite the sight. Sandra with the juice smudged across her face and on her dress. Me hiding my hands in my pockets.

Miss Virginia didn't get cross at us. Instead, she said, "Oh my, look at your pretty dress." She shook her head. She stepped away. "That'll be all for today girls. Now you two go on home."

"But Miss Virginia. What about the black currants?"

"Yes," Sandra said, "We're sorry we didn't wait but they were calling out to us."

Miss Virginia laughed. "I remember when they called out to my sisters and I."

She went all sad again and my stomach did that funny thing. "What about the pictures?"

Miss Virginia asked us to take our places and then said, "Say cheese." After a few photos she asked, "Why are you two so interested in my black currants anyway?"

Sandra whispered in my ear, and we agreed to tell her everything.

"Miss Virginia, we want to earn enough money to exchange friendship bracelets. We saw them at the market, and they cost a quarter a piece," Sandra said.

"The lady at the market makes them herself. She said we could do a friendship ceremony and then we'd be best friends for life."

Miss Virginia didn't speak at first. Instead, she wandered out through the gate, and we followed. She stopped and touched the sunflower faces, like the flowers were old friends. She seemed lost in thought.

I wondered if we were asking too much while offering too little in return.

"Come with me," Miss Virginia said as she began picking dandelions. When her arms were full, she passed some over to Sandra and picked more and passed them over to me. Still not finished, she gathered more and held them in the front of her dress. She sat down and made a pile of the ones she had gathered. She asked us to combine our flowers with hers. We sat down too, Sandra on one side and me on the other.

Miss Virginia picked up a single flower, then another. We watched as she inserted her fingernail into the stems and let the dandelion's milk flow. Although her fingers grew sticky, she continued threading them together creating a string of dandelions. She finished one string then started another.

"You see this milky substance?" Miss Virginia asked. We nodded. "What do you think it is?"

"Is it blood?" Sandra asked.

I wondered about that too but didn't want to say it because I'd never heard of white blood before. I didn't venture to guess and shrugged instead.

"Have you girls heard of latex?"

We shook our heads.

"They use it to make rubber."

"You mean like my India rubber ball?"

"It bounces really high!" Sandra said.

"Yes, girls you've got it. That's why it's so sticky." She continued stringing the flowers together. "We used to make these, my sisters and I when we were your age."

"What happened to them, I mean your sisters?" Sandra asked.

"They're in heaven," she said, as she began a third floral string.

"At least they are together."

Miss Virginia patted my hand. "You're very mature for your age, aren't you? Did you say you just turned seven?"

"I did."

"And you Sandra?"

"I'm seven too."

Miss Virginia stared up at the sky and for a few moments we watched the clouds sailing over us.

"That one looks like a bear," I said, pointing up.

"And that one looks like a big blob of nothing," Sandra said.

We laughed. Miss Virginia had a lovely laugh. "Now, who's first?" she asked, and as I was nearest to her she took my arm. She placed the string of flowers around my wrist and closed the circle: it was a bracelet. She did the same on Sandra's wrist, then closed the third around her own.

"Ah," Miss Virginia said noticing she had quite a few dandelions left. She began stringing them together until she had none left. She stood up. We stood too.

Miss Virginia placed the string of flowers on Sandra's head. "It's called a garland," she said. "Would you like one too?"

"No, thank you," I said.

"I could make a pretty necklace for you?"

I looked at my feet. "I wouldn't want to use up all the dandelions. You need them for wine."

Sandra crossed her eyes and stuck out her tongue.

Miss Virginia paid no attention to Sandra's face-pulling.

"Oh, it's no trouble at all," Miss Virginia said, "I still have some left over from last year," and she began picking. We joined in and with the three of us working together, before long I was wearing a beautiful sunny neckless. When I twirled, it twirled too.

Pleased with our adornments, Sandra and I were in no hurry to depart and spent the afternoon pulling weeds and tidying up the garden.

When it was nearly dinnertime, we said we had to go.

"Wait here just one moment," Miss Virginia said. She returned with a washcloth, a bowl full of water and her pocketbook. "May I?

When Sandra nodded, Miss Virginia dipped the cloth in the water and lifted the stain from Sandra's dress. "It'll dry while you're walking home." She used the washcloth on our hands and our faces.

"Thank you," we said.

"Oh, and one more thing," she reached into her pocketbook and handed us two quarters.

We could buy the friendship bracelets after all!

Without hesitation or consultation, we gratefully declined.

Miss Virginia didn't seem to mind. "See you next year," she said before she closed the front door.

We pulled the empty wagon along the bumpy road, holding the handle carefully so as not to damage our bracelets.

"Maybe next year?" Sandra asked.

"Yeah, maybe next year," I replied. "Now, let's go and get that loaf of bread."

Sandra reached into her pocket. Jingled the change around. "Don't forget the banana popsicle."

Arriving at the corner store we dropped the handle and rushed inside without a thought of Old Lady Macguire.

EPILOGUE

I returned to this street with my teenaged son forty-seven years later and as you can imagine, many things had changed. Some for the good and some not.

The street was no longer dead-end. It was fully paved and widened so there were no more ditches. Most of the houses had been rebuilt with wood and aluminum siding. A few had satellite dishes attached.

Now that the street was open, a new road, lots of houses, a cellular tower and a hydro facility filled the space.

Miss Virginia's house has been torn down and made into units. The back garden has been paved into a parking lot.

Old Lady Macguire's house looks pretty much the same, although the curtains have been replaced with California Shutters.

Sandra and I went our separate ways when her family moved up North. She returned home in 1975, and we went to see the movie, *Jaws*. After that we lost touch.

My red wagon was passed down to my brothers and to my sisters, then on to my cousins. If it could speak, it would have many wonderful tales to tell.

The mere mention of black currants still takes me back to the summer of '67.

THE BRIGHTEST STAR

I T WAS LATE IN the evening, and a young couple stood
under the blanket of the unobstructed night sky. Behind
them a wall of fragrant evergreens guarded the boundaries.

Under the full moon, William and Linda were grounded
by holding hands, even though their eyes and spirits were
consumed by the stars.

The midnight sky stretched its arms open wide above
them. Within the dark night's embrace, they slow danced to
the selected repertoire of the Northern Mockingbird, while
stars and fireflies jostled for attention.

The couple felt like they were the only two living beings
left on earth. Together they were on the edge of the
world, watching listening, married to the sky and after
the Mockingbird winged away, the stimulating sounds of
silence.

Until one solitary star flared up, right out there in front
of them drawing attention to itself. A shooting star. Falling.

Burning a path across the sky. Sizzling, inside an invisible electrical current, speeding, falling.

"Listen, did you hear that?" William asked.

"Yes, it sounded like angels, clapping their wings," Linda replied.

They watched as it advanced, changed courses then disappeared behind a cloud. The experience of seeing it, sharing it, made the couple feel like they were a part of something greater than being, something otherworldly.

We were all born from stardust. Connected forever, both the living and the dead.

When the star was no longer visible, the couple sat down together and waited for something else to happen. Neither spoke, for they were holding the memory, blending feelings and sensations. Framing the moment in their minds forever.

Linda and William knew one thing for certain; nature was the key. On days when everything seemed impossible, when life was unlivable – a spiritual connection to the elements healed them. Gave them hope and elevated their hearts, minds, and bodies.

"Did you make a wish?" Linda asked as a flock of Canada Geeze honked their way across the sky.

"No, I already have you," William replied as he gathered Linda up in his arms. The young couple continued gazing skyward until the geese were no longer seen nor heard.

Linda and William had been through so much together and yet, for each, the other was enough.

"You know, I could sit here forever with you William and let the world go by. I don't feel like I'm missing anything, and I like it when the world is quiet and it's almost like you and I are marooned on an island of our own."

William hugged her ever closer, and Linda now was sitting comfortably on his lap.

As they joined hands a siren rang out in the distance. It broke in upon their little world momentarily until William in a whispered voice began to recite his favourite poem by Walt Whitman:

"When I heard the learn'd astronomer,

When the proofs, the figures, were ranged in columns before me,

When I was shown the charts and diagrams, to add, divide and measure them,

When stirring heard the astronomer where he lectured with much applause in the lecture room

How soon unaccountable I became tired and sick

Till rising and gliding out I wander'd off by myself

In the mystical moist night-air, and from time to time,

Look'd up in perfect silence at the stars." *

A siren screamed in the distance, breaking the moment. Followed by another and a third. The echoes ripped through the calmness, but only for a fleeting time like the star had. One screaming, one burning. Both needing to get somewhere – fast. The first an ugly, harsh sound, a sound signifying danger and chaos. A fellow human being needed help, immediately. The second, a star, beautiful angel wings flapping, dying. Ending.

Such is life and such is death. We all end the same way, no matter how much we scream or how hard we try to make ourselves stand out, to be useful.

The couple remained sitting, totally lost in the moment. Sharing every breath as night unfurled all around them. Crickets chirped and mosquitoes buzzed. The trees groaned, voicing their indignation at the wind for prematurely waking them.

Linda recalled the day when she first met William. In was in high school and they were sixteen years old. Linda was the new kid, from a military family who moved around all the time. Still, she never had trouble fitting in or making friends because she was sweet and pretty and people were drawn to her. The first day she saw William on the football field, she knew he was the one for her. He glanced in her direction, smiled, and sometime later asked her out. Pretty soon they were an item, High school sweethearts. Destined to be together forever.

William was an only child, and his first love was sport. He hoped to get a free ride to one of the best University's on a Football Scholarship after he graduated. When he wasn't practicing, he was playing. He wasn't a scholar, far from it but he admired demanding work, and he was an excellent judge of character. He spotted Linda one day, struggling to open the lock on her locker. He offered to help, but it opened the minute he asked. After that day, he wanted to ask her out, but he didn't until the day they exchanged glances out on the football field. When she smiled at him, he knew she was the one.

Alas their career paths pulled them in different directions. It was a teary good-bye on both of their parts. Both promised to come home every weekend and to stay connected every single day. At first, they texted and called daily, then it changed to every other day, then weekly. It was okay though, because they still came home every weekend, to see each other to be together. The pulling apart and the getting back together again, made them stronger and more connected.

Then something happened, neither knew what it was for certain. Perhaps they were too busy, or perhaps, being apart became the new norm.

Lonely for each other's company but not being able to have it, they started seeing other people. They agreed to see other people, to test the waters, so to speak.

William dated once or twice, but no matter who he saw, all he could think of was Linda. He wondered what she was doing and who she was with. He tried not to care, when people talked about her or saw her on a date, but he did care – he loved her – she was everything to him – but if she was happy, he was man enough to stand back and give her time to figure out what he already knew.

Linda also dated, she was a stunner, and she was smart. She tried to push William and thoughts of him out of her mind. She tried everything, dated guys who were different than William, but there was always something missing. When she heard he was seeing other women, she stuck out her chin and said, "If he can do it then I can do it." One of her friends, who secretly wanted William for herself, spurned her on and Linda continued seeing a guy who she knew wasn't for her. In fact, none of the guys could live up to William because she loved him and only him. Her heart could love no other.

Then she went home, and William was home too, and they ran to each other just like actors did in the movies and swore once they graduated, they'd never to be apart again. And so, it came to pass.

Fifteen years later, still married. Still together.

Even when they lost their jobs. Working at the same company had its advantages, but not when the economy went bad and it was last in first, out. Linda was laid off first, and she scrambled to find another job, but with the baby on the way they decided to stay with the same company with William working full time and having full medical benefits and Linda staying home until their son was old enough to attend Day Care (which the company had on-site.)

Instead of the economy getting better, it got worse and soon William was unemployed too. Both took odd jobs, wherever and whenever they could, divvying up caring for their son as hiring a babysit would be too costly and they needed every penny to continue paying their mortgage.

When there were no jobs to be found, they lost their home. Mortgaged to the hilt, just like all their friends and then, homeless. They lived in their car for a few months, until the creditors tracked them down and repossessed it too.

They stayed together, strong. Clinging to each other.

When they lost their son, it tested everything. No health insurance, no home, no address. A virus, flu, pneumonia and one night, he was gone.

Losing him, nearly drove them over the edge. They teetered and tottered, as the waves of despair dragged them down, and bottles of self-medicating alcohol pulled them up for a few moments then threw them down into the gutter and nearly tore them apart. Now all they had were memories of their boy and a photo framed in a plastic slot in the centre of a pillow which they carried in a backpack with a change of clothes, toiletries, and a roll of toilet paper.

Then they discovered a connection to their son through nature. They walked, higher and higher, feeling his presence in relation to the sky. Not needing sustenance or when they did, finding something in nature. Bathing in the streams, eating apples and wild berries. Dandelions and wild asparagus. Fiddleheads and scallions. Watercress and Northern Wild Rice. All delicacies they were able to forage and to prepare without anything on hand. And water, they sipped the morning dew from the leaves of trees and when it rained, they opened their mouths to the sky and drank their fill.

And they found this spot, high above the city lights. Far from temptation and sound pollution. Surrounded by nature where they could be totally together. In a place where they didn't have to hide from the pain, where nature absorbed it for them, in them.

Where the simplicity of a descending star could captivate them and bring their son back to them in one instant, in the death of a night star.

"We'd better get some sleep, big day tomorrow," William said, as he stretched out his arms and yawned.

"I'd hate to see this one end though."

A rabbit hopped across the grass, stopping now and then to sniff the air. Their stomachs grumbled, but neither was willing to take a life for a feed.

Linda reached into the backpack and pulled out the pillow. She kissed her son's photo and William did the same.

William patted down a spot for himself and then a spot for Linda.

Linda fluffed the pillow. She and placed it on the ground where she rested her cheek upon her son's photo. William did the same.

They snuggled in close together, like two spoons.

Since William was in the back, he carefully unfolded the newspaper pages, A gust of wind zeroed in on them, making its presence known. William held the papers close to his chest, protecting them like they were more valuable than gold.

When the air was calm again, William blanketed Linda with the first and second pages, then took up the slack with overlapping the third and the fourth.

They snuggled in closer. As close as two human beings could ever be.

"Night love," he said.

"Night love," she replied.

FOOTNOTE: *WHEN I HEARD THE LEARN'D ASTRONOMER BY WALT WHITMAN 1865

MARGARET'S REVELATION

S PRING WAS IN THE air. Still Margaret could not pull herself out of the funk.

When feelings overpowered her, Margaret would hug herself because no one else offered to. Her friends said she was copping out. She should speak up. Ask for, no demand what she needed. They said she should not expect her husband to have E.S.P.

In such times, Margaret would roll into an imaginary furry ball, like a mama bear. Then she would stretch and yawn, as if she were waking from a long winter's hibernation.

Have another drink, they would say, as if getting pissed would make things better.

Margaret longed for a new beginning. A seasonal rebirth, one in which she could reconnect to the very core of herself once again.

***

At 5 a.m. in a Toronto West suburb near Lake Ontario, the birds had returned from their winter vacations. A few remained throughout the year – these she considered as her all weather friends. They had already stripped the Huckleberry Bush bare. To bring them back, Margaret filled the feeders with black oil sunflowers seeds.

In winter, the repertoire of bird voices ranged from Blue Jays to Cardinals, to Doves, to Killdeer. Margaret waited in the silence every morning to hear them bring in the new days. Refreshed in body and in mind, she would close her eyes and go back to sleep again. Until disagreeing voices jarred her awake.

It was her teenage son vs. her husband. Although they shared the same blood, their hormones vied for dominance, and they locked horns – especially first thing in the morning.

Margaret and Michael Lindstrom married thirteen years ago and their son, now thirteen, was born not long after. Some said the couple had to get married, but it was none of their damn business.

They had met on a blind date and hit it off straight away. Michael was an executive in the Transport Industry. Margaret was working two jobs while attending College in pursuit of a BA in Graphic Design.

Michael worked long hours. With Margaret studying and covering two jobs, the couple did not see each other often. But when they did, sparks flew. Love was in the air. Total strangers came up to them, commenting how in love they looked, and the sun never failed to shine when they were out walking holding hands.

Margaret's friends were jealous she had a steady boyfriend and concerned. With their busy work schedules, they barely had time for a fling, let alone a full-blown relationship with an older man.

"Just have fun without expectations," Annabelle advised, although she herself to avoid complications had an open-door policy which allowed her to change partners at the drop of a hat.

"But I like him. I mean really like him," Margaret replied.

"If it's meant to be, it can wait until after you graduate," Lizzy, who was in the University game for the long haul, said. She was pursuing a Bachelor of Science Degree in Astrophysics, then moving on to a Master of Science and was still deciding what degree to study for after she graduated. "He's old, but not ancient and unlikely to cark it anytime soon."

He's kind, gentle and thoughtful. Plus, he has invited me on a work gig to meet his colleagues. He says he wants to show me off." She smiled.

"You have enough on your plate already with working two jobs and getting your degree," Annabelle offered. "Not to mention you are way too young to get tied down. Unless the two of you are into that." She scoffed and clinked glasses with Lizzy.

"I could say no, I guess," Margaret said, adding some more wine to her glass.

"Which you don't want to do," Lizzy said. "I say go. Meet all the boring people he works with every day. It'll certainly cure you of any illusions you have of him – if nothing else will."

Margaret sighed and returned to her studies. He was not that old, and he did not act old. A seven-year difference was nothing these days.

Later she went out to dinner with Michael, where she met a few of his work mates. She was closer to their ages than Michael was, but he had a good relationship with everyone and surprisingly, she had an enjoyable time. She liked it when Michael introduced her as his girlfriend. After he said it, he had looked at her like he had expected her to refute it, instead she took his hand. She very much liked being a part of his life.

Not long after the work gig, Michael invited Margaret to join him on an out-of-town business trip. She said no, but then the temptation of visiting Seattle, Washington, made her question her decision. Afterall she could still study and a break from her daily routine would be welcome. If she went, when she came back, she would really hit the books.

"It's all expenses paid," Michael coerced. "I'll be out during the day… you'll have plenty of time to study–by the pool–in the hot tub."

She shook her head no, but he could tell she was weakening.

"And we're flying Business Class."

Well, that did it. She packed a bag and off they went to Seattle where, by day, she studied. By night they watched the Mariners play one night, went to the Tractor Tavern Rock Club on another. They heard Bill Clinton do a talk at the Seattle Centre. They went up the Space Needle and took in the sights of Chihuly Garden and went to the Museum of Pop Culture. It was like they were on their honeymoon; love was in the air. and they conceived Tommy.

Margaret and Michael had not talked about children. Margaret did not know how to approach the subject. She considered having an abortion, but it was not in her to hurt someone who didn't choose to be born. She invited Michael out to dinner and broached the subject.

"I want a family, lots of kids," he said.

She smiled.

"I don't see myself as the marrying type though," he paused. "However, if there was a child involved, I'd consider getting married. All kids deserve the best start possible."

"I think I'm pregnant," she blurted.

He was quiet at first, then jumped up and hugged her. He said they needed to know for certain. She made an appointment to see her doctor. When he confirmed what she already knew, they clung to each other crying like idiots. Even now when she thought about that day, she had to fight back the tears.

She dropped out of college when morning sickness took over her life. Missed classes seemed to stack up. When it was clear, she would need to repeat the entire year, Margaret took a sabbatical and concentrated all she had on the future. There was plenty to do before the baby arrived. They sold his apartment. Bought a house in the burbs and had a quick wedding at the Registry Office to make it all official.

The soon to be new mother spent her days making their home homey. When they found out they were having a boy, Margaret went full speed ahead with creating a wonderful nursery. They chose a sports theme, baseball, hockey, basketball. Even soccer. All sport activities which she and Michael enjoyed watching on their flat screen tv.

When Michael was at work, sometimes Margaret made a tray of foods like ice cream, celery, mushrooms, and salsa. Then she would plunk herself in front of the television, put on some. soothing music for the baby and read to him. Margaret had lost track of how many times she had read What to Expect When You're Expecting to her little one. To her, it was like a baby bible and sharing knowledge further strengthened their connection.

One sunny afternoon, she went to the local second-hand bookstore with a list of the favourite books she had loved as a little girl. She had forgotten to ask Mark what his favourite books were, but he never was much of a reader. It took two trips to bring all the books inside. She sat on the loveseat, with the boxes of books in front of her. She could not believe she had found them all! Even the Pokey Little Puppy which was the first book she had ever learned to read herself. Oh, and she flipped through copies of Charlotte's Web, Anne of Green Gables, Curious George, The Bobbsey Twins, Heidi, and the entire Harry Potter series. Mark laughed and said they'd better invest in a bookshelf. He did better than that, he built one himself saying there would be none of that mumbo jumbo furniture in his son's bedroom.

Soon enough, Tommy arrived, and he was the most beautiful piece of art she had ever seen. At times she could not believe that she and Michael had created him. Her heart grew, she never knew she could love anyone more than she loved Michael: and she loved him a lot.

Michael wanted to have another baby straight away, but a second pregnancy was not in the cards. Tommy's birth had been a difficult one, and the doctor advised them not to try again. Michael agreed it wasn't worth the risk, and he was fine with it, or so he said. Margaret did not believe him, although he had always been honest in the past.

Loud noises downstairs erupted again, pulling Margaret out of her head and back to reality. Tommy shouted first, slamming a cupboard, then Michael told him off and things escalated quickly. They butted heads over the most ridiculous topics. Neither were morning people…nor was she.

Just one simple morning of peace and quiet was all she needed to get herself back on track.

Margaret considered getting up, then rejected the notion. She would wait until they asked for her help. Inevitably, they would ask.

Tommy popped his head into her room. Instead of keeping his voice down, he shouted, "Are you asleep, Mom?" He would wait for a second or two for her to stir.

"Yes," she always replied, rubbing her tired eyes even though sleeping through the raucous would be impossible.

Now that he had her attention he would cry out, "I can't find my sport shirt, Mom."

She smiled since she always put them in the exact same place, but she did not mention it this time. What was the point? "They're in your closet, love."

"They are soooo, NOT!" he said, followed by a stomp, a retreat, and a door slam.

She started counting one Mississippi, two Mississippi, three Mississippi.

"Found it! Thanks, Mom! It WAS right here all the time."

Margaret would settle back down under the covers and drift off to sleep once again. Until her husband Michael returned to their room. He followed a strict regime. First there was toilet, then handwashing, teeth brushing, flossing, tongue scraping with intermittent and very audible gagging sounds (which often made her cover her ears with the pillow.) Followed by a fifteen-minute shower, shave, more teeth brushing, blow drying, primping, cologne. Everything timed to the second.

When he was finished, he threw the door open wide and the hot steam would escape before he did into the room. She would watch him crossing the floor like he was following a fleeing ghost. The smell of his cologne and the warm steam made her sleepy and soon she would fall asleep again.

"Margaret, have you seen a stray cufflink?"

She would pop her head up, "Not lately," she would reply as he riffled through the top drawer without closing it all the way. Then he would open the middle drawer, leaving it partially open. Finally, the bottom drawer pulled all the way out. The armoire resembled a staircase, but it was a hazard since it could easily topple over at any moment. She imagined Tommy walking by and the entire chest of drawers landing on top of him. The terror of what might happen tore her to the core. If she had to get him out from underneath… did she have the strength? What if… She jumped out of bed and closed each drawer.

"I was going to do it," Michael said as he slammed the door behind him on the way out.

Since she was already up, she would press herself against the back of the closed door until from downstairs Tommy called, "Mom, I can't find my lunch!"

"It's in your lunch box, second shelf, right-hand side of the fridge."

"No, it's not," he replied.

"Coming," she said as she gripped the door handle but before she had the time to open it he called, "Oh, I see it now! Thanks, Mom."

Returning to her room, mumbled you're welcome, as the black gap beneath the bed beckoned. She could slide right under there with nothing to keep her company except for the dust bunnies. Under there, she would create her very own superpower – a protective shield of darkness which repelled loud angry voices.

Voices coming nearer made the decision for her and she scrambled into the dark space. In the cozy environment, her breathing and heartbeat slowed. She closed her eyes, flattened herself out, then reaching up with her hand, she pulled the quilt down to the floor and dragged it under and over her entire body like she had built a fort.

Michael returned to their room. "Hon?" he said.

Tommy paused at the door, "Maybe she's in the bathroom?"

Michael checked, then glanced at the bed.

"She's not under there again, is she?" Tommy whispered.

"Let's see," she heard Michael reply.

The two lowered themselves to the ground and peeked into the darkness. Saw some movement under the blanket. Michael looked at his son, then put his finger to his lips. He nodded, happy to let his father speak first.

"Hon," Michael said, in a soothing voice, "Would you mind taking my pants and shirts to the dry cleaners?" He opened his mouth then closed it again.

Poor Margaret could not believe he was giving her a to do list and talking to her like she hid under the bed every single day of her life. It annoyed the shit out of her.

Not getting the hint, he continued, "Oh, and I forgot to ask you on the weekend, uh, if it was okay for me to invite a few friends over. Tonight. For a little shindig. A party of eight, including us. Sorry for such short notice again. Meant to ask you on the weekend."

Tommy made a move to join his mother in her solitary cocoon. Instead, she limbo-ed her way out. Straightening up, she dusted herself off. They were staring at her, but not saying anything. "You two go on down, now," she said still hold the warm duvet.

Michael glanced at his watch.

"I'm fine, perfectly fine. I'll be there in a minute, please." She put the quilt back onto the bed.

"Okay," they answered, leaving.

When they were gone, she reached across the bed. She turned off the electric blanket on her husband's side. As she put her housecoat and slippers on, she imagined forgetting to turn his blanket off. Would the house burn down? Probably. And it would be her fault. Everything was always her fault.

She closed her housecoat, then fixed her hair in the mirror. She had to talk to Michael about the dinner party. Eight people. Tonight. At least it was not as bad as the last time when there were twelve, or the time before when there had been eighteen. Still, she had asked him so many times on other occasions like this one to give her more notice. The last time she had completed everything – well, nearly everything – she did not have time to varnish her nails. Michael pointed this out awkwardly in front of the guests and even their son had enough emotional intelligence to change the subject before she burst into tears.

In the hallway, her bunny slippers made sparks as she walked, giving her shocks as she picked up socks, underwear, and a cufflink along the way. Bits and pieces left for her like a trail to lead her downstairs to where they were waiting.

Downstairs now, she stood in the hallway leading to the living room. As she stepped inside, she saw and heard her husband crunching on toast while holding a cup of tea pinky aloft. Beside him was Tommy, scarfing down Rice Crisps and missing his mouth. Droplets of milk and cereal debris gathered between his feet, making pitter-patter sounds as they hit the carpet.

She made a mental note to toss the rug into the dryer after they'd gone, relieved that the fabric on the floor was mopping up the liquid rather than staining what she believed to be her son's last clean school shirt. She added a second mental note to order him some new shirts – he was growing so fast; it was hard to keep up with the growth spurts.

"Good morning," Margaret said just as Fred Flintstone yelled, Wilma!

Her family acknowledged her presence by glancing in her direction, then together burst into laughter as Barney and Fred carried on with their usual antics. At least they were getting along. The Flintstones was one thing they both agreed on.

When there was a commercial break she said, "About this dinner party, Michael." He turned down the volume on the set. Tommy protested, then finished eating his cereal.

"Sorry about that again," her husband said. "I was talking to my boss on the weekend at the golf game. Not sure how it ended up being here, but the next thing I knew, I was hosting the bloody event. Does not have to be black tie or anything fancy. Three courses, plus dessert should do."

"Who are our guests? What kinds of food do they like? Any allergies? Any vegetarians?" She paused. "Why don't we fire up the grill?"

"Nah, the grill idea is great for a weekend get together, but this is business motivated."

She sighed.

He continued, "My boss and his wife, Jim and Dave from marketing, Lucy, and her husband William from legal. I think Lucy might be vegetarian or vegan. Lance in finance and his wife – have not met her before. He's new on our team." He glanced at his watch and jumped.

Margaret caught hold of his sleeve. She inserted the missing cufflink, then wedged herself directly in front of her husband in hope of receiving a kiss.

Michael hesitated for a second before he gave Margaret what some might qualify as a kiss – she did not. It was more like a peck –administered on the fly – as he zipped by. The couple's lips had barely touched.

Before Margaret could get a word out, Mark slammed the door behind him.

She wrapped her arms around herself again. For a second or two it looked like Tommy was going to give her a hug. She opened her arms, and he in returned extended his arm in her direction open palm facing up. She crossed her arms, as he went straight into Sales Pitch 101.

"You see Mom, today is Burger Day – two for one – and I need money. The money is for charity, and I've already spent all my pocket money this week."

"What about the lunch I made?"

"No problem, I'll eat it at Recess."

Margaret patted him on the head and then went into the kitchen where her purse was hanging on the hook. As she reached inside, she glanced at the state of her kitchen. What a mess! And she had to get everything spic and span for a dinner party this evening. No problem!

She only had a ten-dollar bill, which she placed into his still waiting hand. "Bring me change," she said as he left the house with a firm slam of the door.

Back in the living room The Flintstones were wrapping up with, "You'll have a gay old time!" Margaret hummed along while she threw the rug over her shoulder, gathered up the dirty cup and saucer, glass, and bowl.

Now in the kitchen, she put the rug into the washing machine, the breakfastware into the dishwasher, then she poured herself a cup of tea from the lukewarm pot. She returned to the living room, which was less of a mess. She flicked through the channels and came across Judge Judy. She could not help but admire the woman, who had total control of everyone and everything in her court room.

Her friends said she should get up before her family did, that would minimize the chaos and the mess. She would be at the helm of the situation then. Others said, she should get a job and leave the house before they did, so they would have to learn to fend for themselves. She was so tired though, so un-herself these days, not to mention she had not worked since before her son was born. Who would hire her now?

Margaret had grown increasingly dissatisfied with her lot, as she surrendered her life for the needs of those she loved. She resented the always giving, although it was her choice to do so. Then she would climb on the guilt and self-pity train. Did every mother go through the same thing? This emptiness? This pushing and pulling within herself, creating a void. This emptiness within, which she allowed to move like a summer storm and rain upon everything in her life. She was a hurricane waiting to happen and today was the day she had been dreading.

She showered and dressed, without stopping for breakfast but taking time to toss the rug into the dryer, and with a fervent desire to get out. Away. Anywhere, away.

Margaret pointed her car in the direction of the mall and drove. Parked. On the way inside, a young man was shepherding trolleys. With the help of the wind, several were destined for imminent escape. She considered saying something to ease the man's burden, instead she smiled at him. Under his breath he called her a bitch.

The housewife ignored him and hurried inside. She could not help but wonder why her empathetic gesture had achieved nothing but abuse. Never mind, she thought, shifting her focus to the problem at hand: dinner party preparations. First things first, though: what was she going to wear? Should she treat herself to a new outfit? Shopping had helped lift her spirits in the past. Perhaps it would do the trick today?

Margaret made her way along the fashion corridor, finding a mannequin in a window display wearing a posh suit which she liked. She ventured inside, where mirrors everywhere assaulted her. She retreated.

On the escalator, she noticed a hair and nail spa. She glanced at her nails. She preferred to do them herself at home once she knew what she would be wearing – she would make time. But her hair, that was another matter.

She stood outside the salon, watching stylists moving about, keeping themselves busy. It appeared to be a quiet day in the salon, since only one chair was occupied. She considered going in, talking to someone but decided against it as she glanced at her phone. Time was ticking away, and she had way too much to do already.

A flashing neon sign attracted her attention. It read:

Travel to your dream destination. Sale Today Only!

No longer Margaret, she was Margarita in Cuba. She imagined herself in Cuba performing the rhumba. Then she was in Australia, dancing in the Outback. No way! It was way too far away.

A young man about half her age noticed her. "I'll be with you in a moment," he said. He returned to his conversation on the phone.

She ventured inside and stood awkwardly near the front desk. She listened to the young man's calm voice. Sometimes he acknowledged her presence with a smile. After a few moments, he stopped talking and cupped his hand over the phone.

"Help yourself to a cup of coffee or water while you wait. I won't be long. Oh and feel free to browse through the brochures and magazines. I'll be right with you."

Margaret poured herself a steaming hot cup of coffee, then added cream and a lump of sugar. She glanced in the direction of the young man on the phone when she noticed a box of biscuits. Like she was seeking his permission.

He cupped his hand over the receiver again, "Oh, yes, do help yourself to a biscuit or two. You're very welcome."

"Thank you," she whispered, picking up a biscuit. It was chocolate heaven.

While she waited, she flipped through some magazines. The first one was about Switzerland. Now she was Maggie preparing to ski at the Zermatt with tall, blond, and handsome ski instructor named Sven helping her with her skis. Now they finished skiing, and he was offering her a hot cup of cocoa. She swooned and reached for it, then blinked him away.

She picked up another brochure for Hawaii, imagining herself on the beach in Waikiki, hula-ing with George Clooney. Then she looked down, realizing she was wearing a bikini and screamed.

Margaret snapped back to reality, glancing in the direction of the young man who was still on the phone. He hadn't noticed her outburst. Whew. She took another bite of the chocolate biscuit. Wearing a bikini or any other kind of bathing suit was out of the question.

On the wall, she spotted a poster advertising a trip to Britain. Beefeaters. Wearing those crazy tall hats. Now she was Cathy, looking for Heathcliff on the Yorkshire Moors. It was a very cold and windy day, but they were walking and enjoying the fresh air...

"May I help you?" the young man asked.

Heathcliff disappeared. "Uh, just dreaming," Margaret replied with flushed cheeks.

The young man clicked on his keyboard, looking at the screen. He turned the computer toward her. "These are today's one-day only last-minute deals. They just came in!"

Intrigued, she moved closer.

"If you're interested in England, you won't find a price like this again."

"I've always wanted to visit the U.K."

"This price," the young man said, "Includes a rental car, and a combination of hotels and B&Bs. You could travel around, then choose where you wanted to stop and stay."

"I don't know about driving there, don't they drive on the other side?"

"That's true, but you'll pick it up in no time."

***

Margaret returned home and placed a takeout order. She chose a variety of dishes from the menu to suit every need. She put the Chardonnay, Rose, and beer into the refrigerator. The four bottles of red she placed into the wine rack.

She tied an apron around her waist, then got down to vacuuming and dusting. She repositioned the clean rug in the living room. When everything was perfect, she set the table with places for seven at the table. Michael would not want to risk Tommy causing a scene. Not in front of his boss and work mates. She prepared a tray and set it up on the counter so he could take it to his room.

Margaret went into her room and packed a suitcase and a carry-on bag. She ordered an Uber to drop her off at the airport.

Three hours later, she boarded a plane and was soon winging her way to the United Kingdom.

As she looked out the window, for a split second a pang of guilt overcame her. She fought it.

She had left a note on the fridge that said she was going away.

Margaret had failed to mention where she was going or when she would return.

Nor, that she had purchased a one-way ticket. They would figure it out.

THE UMBRELLA AND THE WIND

I T WAS FRIDAY THE 13th, and the wind was whipping around. Things which weren't meant to fly were bouncing and ricocheting. Across and over. Somersaulting all around me.

On such a day some retired persons might have remained in bed, but not I. Why should I venture out, on such a dreadful day? For this reason and this reason alone — I needed a strong cup of coffee.

Consequently, I played dodgem, ducking, and diving to get myself out of the house and into my car. Then I made my way toward the nearest drive-through. I wasn't the only one brave enough to venture into the unknown to cure my caffeine addiction.

The queue moved forwards, inching along. I placed my order for an Extra Strong Vanilla Latte then car crawled my way toward the window to pay. I reached across for my wallet and discovered I'd left it at home.

The lady at the window, reached out her hand and pulled it back in again to avoid a small branch which contacted my window then bounced into hers.

"Change," I said, as the woman reached out again. I was still rifling through the glove compartment and cup slots. After counting I had seventy-eight cents. Under my seat was another dollar. I continued searching, while the cars behind me waited and the guy directly behind me honked, others following.

"That'll do," the woman said, as she took the coins and handed me the coffee.

I smiled my biggest smile and said, "Thank you," I closed the window and pulled away, ever so grateful. The coffee smelled like heaven, but I held off taking a sip until the first red light.

As I waited, sipping, savoring, an unhumanned umbrella cracked my windshield with its wooden handle before bouncing away and coming to rest on a nearby tree branch.

I didn't even realize the java was burning me until the light changed. I pulled over safely and stepped out of the vehicle. Nothing like hot coffee running down your leg into your socks and shoes. I shook my leg, like a dog who'd recently had a bath.

I saw it coming, but it was too late.

That damned umbrella. Again.

***

I woke up, still in the parking lot with the wooden umbrella handle wrapped around my neck. I'd fallen hard but managed to grab hold of the car door on the way down, which was a good thing in one way and bad in another since it hid my predicament.

The concrete below me felt cold and spongy. I tried to stand up, and the wind caught the umbrella, carrying on its journey like a wayward tumbleweed.

I wasn't standing yet but launched myself upwards pushing my weight against the car door. The sudden click of the door lock did not bode well for me — I had left the keys in the ignition. I felt around for my phone, quickly realizing it was at home with my handbag.

I leaned against the car with crossed arms in the hope of attracting a Good Samaritan.

In the distance, I spotted the umbrella as it made its way elsewhere. Oops. An oncoming vehicle trying to avoid the whirling dervish slammed into the back of another car. Someone would call the police now. I'd wave them over to help me, too. All good.

Before long, the damned umbrella was off again, hurtling at full speed in my direction. Was I an umbrella magnet? It flew up high this time, spinning. It was a thing of beauty in the distance. It opened to the sky in all its blackness. It was mesmerizing, so high up it went, and you know the old saying, 'What goes up,' well, it was proving to be true as the damn thing plummeted to the ground with the potential of knocking me out for good. Like the Boy Scout motto, I was prepared and instead of waiting for it to connect with my head, I reached out and grabbed it by the handle.

I held on for dear life, hoping not to Mary Poppins myself. My feet did leave the ground, but only for a second or two before I heard sirens and shoes slapping on the pavement.

A young woman closed her hand over mine on the handle. We steadied ourselves, as more footsteps walked the streets as its owner clicked the button and closed the collapsible canopy.

***

After the strange morning, I went home and put my feet up, refusing to budge until the wind let up. I kept to the plan until my son asked me to pick him up just past 7:30 at his friend's place across town. The parents were meant to bring him home, but they were nervous drivers, hence my summoning.

The bull's eye crack on my windshield was a constant reminder of how my day was going thus far. I was still waiting for word from my insurance company about the deductible. They were investigating the 'act of god' angle.

I contacted the police who said they would verify the existence of the umbrella but not that it connected with my windshield. When they saw me, I was holding onto it.

Feeling extremely cross at the person who had failed to keep a hold of their canopy of cloth I had half a mind to write to the council to request an Umbrella License Policy. Then I could make them pay my deductible, or even better, sue.

I started the car and backed out of the driveway, conscious of flying objects, when a green bottle caught my eye. It was spinning and spinning around in a circle, like imaginary people playing a game of Spin the Bottle. It didn't leave the ground most of the time and looked like an oblong green spaceship as it took off, lifted higher and higher, then crashed, spun, and lifted again. I continued, coincidentally in the same direction the bottle was heading.

When I saw a man and a woman walking toward each other while the bottle was perilously somersaulting, I opened my window and called out to them. When they didn't react, I honked my horn. The bottle, now high up in the air began to freefall toward them.

The bottle came down, hitting the woman's head with full force. The green container then ricocheted and connected with the man's head. The indifferent green object rose and fell several times before coming to a stop against the trunk of a tree.

I put my four-way flashers on and turned the engine off before stepping out from the safety of my car into the hazardous wind once again.

Both the man and the woman were conscious, however they weren't moving around or trying to stand up. I took the woman's pulse, then the man's and assessed the situation, remembering my First Aid training from years ago. I dialed 911. The dispatcher asked a few questions, but the cracking behind us made the people sit up.

We watched as the wind continued to roar, sending the bottle flying. The majestic weeping willow bent over to reclaim it, but too late. The wind snapped its thick torso in half and as the tree hit the ground the reverberations rocked the earth beneath us.

"Come on!" I shouted.

With the wind snapping at our heels, we made a break for it.

***

Once we reached the sanctuary of my car and buckled in, I floored it. With the bottle no longer in sight we drove on to collect my son.

After a few moments of catching our breaths, we introduced ourselves.

Brent Welch was a tall and very handsome man, with dark hair and blue eyes. He had a dimple on his chin like Cary Grant. He was a partner with a local law firm, very well spoke, noticeably lovely manners and he was single.

Eileen Manny, also single, had long blonde hair and wore too much makeup. She was a reserved and soft-spoken cosmetic representative so her 'face was her pallet.'

I introduced myself. "My name is Alice Mitchell. I'm recently widowed and a retired high school teacher."

Now that we were acquainted, they thanked me for rescuing them. Then they asked about the crack in the windshield just as Jasper clambered into the vehicle and buckled in.

After introductions, I continued to tell the umbrella story. My passengers roared with laughter.

"What's so funny?" I asked.

"It couldn't have happened to anyone else," Jasper replied.

We set off home, dropping Mark and Eileen along the way.

When we finally made it, I realized there were still two hours remaining on this more than eventful Friday the 13th. I climbed into bed, pulled the covers over my head, and tried to sleep.

I had no idea what was still to come.

***

The next morning, Saturday the 14th, it took me a few minutes to wake up. It was like the doorbell was ringing in my dream until my son Jasper knocked on my bedroom door.

"Mom it's for you — the cops."

I threw back the covers, pulled my nightgown over my head, replaced it with a jogging suit and finger brushed my hair before stepping out.

My son, who has little etiquette about these things even though he was raised with excellent manners, had left the officers standing on the front porch.

As I poked my head outside, half in and half out, the wind picked up and nearly pulled the door out of my hands.

The officers' appearance was disheveled which in the old days used to be referred to as 'windswept and interesting.' The burly pair of officers were handsome enough to moonlight as strippers from the Thunder from Down Under. I invited them in.

"No thank you, ma'am," the blond-haired guy, who when he removed his hat looked like the other guy, the one who wasn't 'Ponch' from C.H.I.P.S., said.

'Jon,' I said aloud without meaning to (the name of the blond guy from C.H.I.P.S. had just occurred to me.)

"The name is Marshall," the blond one said. "My partner is Officer Ramsey."

"Pleased to meet you. And what can I do for you?"

Blondie said, "We received a report of an abandoned 911 call from you yesterday, can you please explain what happened?"

"I observed a man and a woman walking toward each other while waiting for a red light to change. I noticed the bottle."

"In mid-flight?" Ramsey asked.

I nodded. "Yes, the bottle went up and then came back down again. I tried to attract their attention, but before I knew it the bottle hit the woman first and then the man. Both went down on the sidewalk, hard."

"What state were they in when you reached them and how long did it take for you to get there?" Jon, I mean Marshall, asked.

"I parked within seconds and went to their side immediately."

Ramsey was the note guy; he was writing down everything I said.

Marshall had his phone pointed at me; he was recording everything I said.

I guessed it was okay, although I didn't question it at the time.

"They were conscious, breathing and with strong pulses. After confirming this, I called 911."

"What happened then?"

"A huge tree came crashing down and we made a run for it to my car."

"Did either of them ask to see a doctor or go to Emergency?"

"No, they were wide awake. We were laughing and talking. Their houses were on the way back. We dropped them off and it was no trouble at all."

We remained silent.

***

"What's this all about?" I asked, feeling the wind cutting through my track suit.

"Have you ever met either of them before?" Marshall asked. "After all, their houses aren't far away from yours."

"No." I stood quietly, trying to figure out where they were going with their questions. What did it matter whether I had seen either of them? Inside my son turned on the television and the sounded blasted. I closed the door behind me and stepped out.

"What kind of a bottle was it?" Ramsey asked.

"It was a green bottle."

The two officers exchanged glances.

"Is it true you had another incident yesterday involving an umbrella?" Marshall asked.

"Yes, it was a terrible Friday the 13th."

"Thing is," Ramsey said. "Welch and Manny died."

***

I woke up from having fainted with three worried faces peering down at me. Two belonged to Officers Ramsey and Marshall. In their hands they held copies of Reader's Digest which they waved at me like fans. The other belonged to Jasper, who held a glass of water from which he intermittently splayed droplets onto my forehead.

"Are you okay, Mom?"

I wasn't one hundred percent certain. Still, I tried to sit up to avoid any more of the Reader's Digest and water assaults.

"You had a bit of a shock," Ramsey said, just as two ambulance attendants made their way over to me. One checked my pulse, the other snapped on the blood pressure band and started pumping. Both said, "All good."

I attempted to escort them to the door, but they said it wasn't necessary.

Ramsey sat opposite me.

The butterflies in my stomach were fluttering around, and I was still feeling a bit delicate as questions about flying bottles killing people floated around in my head.

I thought I was only thinking the last thought until Ramsey answered, "We don't know the cause of death yet. The coroner is examining the bodies."

"We noticed you have a big crack in your windshield," Marshall said. "Did either of them run into it?"

"No, it was caused by the umbrella."

"I think we have enough information," the officers said.

Jasper showed them out.

I went into the kitchen, made myself a strong cup of tea and opened a packet of chocolate biscuits. Outside, I could hear the wind as it blew the leaves around and around. I opened the back door and asked Mother Nature to cease and desist.

As expected, she ignored my request.

***

Sunday was a quiet day. I kept to myself, and Jasper treated me like it was Mother's Day with breakfast, lunch, and dinner in bed. Still in shock, I happily accepted the role of the invalid for one day and one day only.

Monday morning first thing I made my way to the glass replacement shop. All I had to do was pay the deductible and they would fix it on the spot.

My phone rang, and it was Officer Ramsey. He asked me to come down to the station, "And bring your car."

I explained where I was and why. He said my car was "under investigation." He said I'd be carless for a couple of days.

I told him I'd be there as soon as possible and left the premises.

Later, I was waiting at a red light when I noticed a young couple walking together holding hands. In his other hand was a cup of coffee. She was drinking from a green bottle. One moment they were happy, next moment she dropped his hand like it was a hot potato. He in turn dropped his hot coffee and it spilled all over his trousers and shoes.

In a flash of a second, he hit the bottom of her bottle, and it flew up into the air. Those of us waiting at the lights saw it go up. It was like a rocket, soaring straight up sky high.

It came down just as the young couple looked up.

It hit the woman's head first, ricocheted off the man's noggin, and rolled along the pavement into the street.

I was out of my car like a shot, dialing 911 on the way. Others followed me, getting out of their vehicles. We blocked the entire intersection.

The girl was unconscious, and the man was wide awake.

"An ambulance is on the way," I said.

We heard the sirens. Saw the police cars.

"What on earth are you doing here?" Ramsey asked.

"Oh boy," I replied.

***

I explained the situation. There were plenty of witnesses this time.

After the ambulance put the couple inside and screamed off, the officers told everyone to clear the area, except for me. They had already spoken to most of the witnesses.

"Are you arresting me?"

They exchanged glances.

"Do you still need to impound my vehicle?" I was showing off, I'd seen plenty of police shows.

"You can head on home," Ramsey said.

"We know where you live," Marshall said with a smirk. "Just don't leave town, okay?"

I laughed and went on my way.

***

There were no incidents on the way home.

I put the roast chicken into the oven, peeled the potatoes. and cut up some veggies, all the while thinking about airborne green bottles.

I went into my office and typed 'flying bottles' into a search engine. It linked me to a guy on YouTube who put candy inside a bottle, then smashed it on the ground. Nothing happened. Intrigued, I continued watching. The next time he smashed it, the bottle after connecting with the face of a camera man launched into the air like a rocket.

Then I came across some Myth Busters experiments which confirmed that a full bottle had the potential to crack a skull. On the contrary, empty bottles could not — that myth had been truly busted by the two recent deaths.

I turned off the computer. I didn't want to think about this anymore.

On cue, Jasper came in. "Everything okay Mom?"

I told him about latest incident and the experiments on YouTube.

"You are joking, right?"

I shook my head and went into the kitchen to stir the potatoes.

"To top it off, the officers called to the scene were Ramsey and Marshall. They must think I'm some kind of a jinx."

"It's a small-town Mom, we're all in each other's business. Did anyone record the incident on their phones?"

Out of the mouths of babes. If they had, it might have been loaded online. "How do I find it? What key words should we use?"

We went back into my office and sure enough there it was.

"You need to tell the officers."

Officer Ramsey answered straightaway. Jasper sent him the direct link while I filled him in on the details.

The potatoes were nearly finished, so I poured out the water and added some salt and pepper.

Jasper and I sat down to dinner with the television sound in the background. There was an update on the couple hit by the bottle. We put down our cutlery and moved closer. The announcer said the girl's condition was critical, but thankfully the boy was stable.

We weren't hungry anymore.

***

I didn't sleep much, kept tossing and turning.

Eventually I gave in and made myself a cup of tea.

I stood, holding it, looking out the window at the wind which was still blowing and swirling things around. I shivered.

In my life, good things and terrible things always happened in threes.

I went into my office and clicked on some information about supernatural happenings including forebodings. All the signs were there. The universe was trying to tell me something.

But what?

The signs suggested it could be an angry spirit, someone who had been murdered or killed before their time.

Someone who was hanging around, seeking vengeance. I couldn't see any connection to the victims. They were after all total strangers.

I began typing furiously. Making lists always helped me to figure things out.

In column number one, I put myself. Single. Widowed. Retired. One son. Married for thirty-five years. Husband died of colon cancer. Stage 4. Both of my parents were deceased. I was an only child. Our family had always lived locally. Our genealogy went way back in this area.

In list number two I put Brent Welch. He was thirty-three years of age and was a lawyer. I googled his obituary. He was single. Never married. Lived alone. His family lineage went way back in this area too. How had we never met? His relatives were instrumental in turning our community into a habitable place way back in the days of pioneering. His mother and father were both deceased. He was an only child.

We had a few things in common. That made me sit up.

In the next column I put Eileen Manny. She was thirty-nine years old. Had a twin sister named Esther who lived locally. So much for that theory. They had local roots, but they didn't go back as far as Brent and mine. Eileen was married, but her husband had passed. Eileen's parents were both alive, but they moved away. Eileen's daughter attended the same school as Jasper. Odd we hadn't crossed paths before.

My lists contained little information and were absolutely no help.

Sleepy now, I went back to bed where lists of useless information swirled around in my head.

***

It was raining extremely hard, but the clouds weren't in their normal places. Instead, they were below me. It was raining, from the ground up. Another sign of climate change and urban pollution?

I floated outside of myself, while my feet remained firmly planted inside my Tender Tootsies. My legs were hidden under a flowered multi-colored skirt, sixties style. It blew in the wind, exposing them, as the skirt accordioned out then back in again. On my waist was a belt of very thick, brown leather. It was too tight, constricting me.

Was I dead?

I pinched myself. So not dead.

I was wearing a white blouse with a high frilly collar and a necklace, beads, black, a rosary. I ran the cool beads through my fingers trying to braille it all out, but I couldn't remember what to do with it.

The wind picked me up, carried me. Blew me forwards and backwards.

My long hair snaked down my back in one tight braid.

I stood upon a piece of land then, above the clouds. There wasn't a huge amount of space to move around without fear of falling.

"Mom! Mom! Wake up! Wake up please."

It was Jasper. I was back.

I screamed as a green fireball singed my hair and melted the rosary. It dripped down my chest and through my fingers.

***

I sat up and looked at my fingers, expecting to see green gobs seeping through, but they were as clean as a whistle. It had been nothing but a bad dream.

My son was still calling out for me. I ran to the living room and opened and closed my eyes a couple of times to reassure myself that I was seeing what I was seeing. What a mess!

A green thing had crashed through the roof of my house. On the way down to its final resting place (the basement) it had smashed and destroyed everything in its path while spraying a neon green substance around my home like a dog marking its territory. The shade of green might have been a nice touch, if there hadn't been so much of it and if it hadn't been spattered about in a random fashion.

"What on earth?"

"Didn't you hear it?" Jasper asked. "It was like a sonic boom."

I walked closer to the hole. I hadn't heard a thing. I'd been sleeping, dreaming. Now I was wide awake and speechless. I crossed my arms and looked down. Steam was rising from it. I stretched out the palm of my hand and even though it was a floor below us, I could feel the heat rising. I tried to speak but there were no words.

Jasper watched, waited for me to say something.

It didn't look like much of anything, embedded into my basement floor. It wasn't round, square, or egg-shaped. It had many faces, was three dimensional, spherical, almost Euclidean, a solid dodecahedron.

"Shouldn't we call someone?" Jasper asked as he leaned over the edge beside me.

"Not sure who we should call. We're not hurt; it's the house that is. It's not a ghost so The Ghost Busting team wouldn't help. I'm not sure if Neil deGrasse Tyson or any of the Science magazines make house calls."

Jasper laughed. "I sure wish Stephen Hawking was still around."

"I think this is more like a Stephen King thing," I said.

We were in a state of shock but holding it together with humor.

"We need to go down there and take a closer look."

"I don't know, Mom; the thing is radiating heat. I feel like I'm getting a sun burn just standing here."

He was right, but I hadn't noticed because hot flashes at my age were the norm.

"What about the police?" Jasper asked, pulling out his phone and taking a few photos.

"Not sure how they could help, but at least they are within driving distance." I dreaded the idea of speaking with Officers Ramsey and Marshall.

"I took this," Jasper showed me, "as it came through the roof."

The photo of the thing in downward motion displayed it folding and unfolding right before it hit.

"It's distorted," Jasper said. "It was moving really fast."

I dialed the police department and Officer Ramsey had the day off, so I asked for Officer Marshall. After I explained he asked, "Is this a joke?"

Having sent a photo before, I sent one to him now. Proof. I waited.

Officer Marshall asked if anyone was hurt, and I confirmed it was only the house. I explained our intention to go downstairs and take a closer look. He suggested we wait for him and check it out together.

After hanging up, Jasper and I went into the kitchen, and I put on the kettle.

"Of all the houses in the world, why ours?" he asked.

"Was just thinking the same thing son." I was also thinking about the insurance company and what they were going to say. First the broken windshield and now a demolished house. I poured water into the instant coffee, and we sat down.

"If it was made of jade, we'd be stinking rich," Jasper said.

"Yes, the Chinese call Jade the Gemstone of Heaven."

We sipped and walked around looking down, the heat pouring from it. Rising. I wondered if it might be hot enough to set the rest of the house on fire. I decided to call the fire department.

***

Our doorbell started ringing with unexpected guests shortly thereafter. It wasn't the officers or the fire department. It was our neighbors. They heard the crash, gathered, and came to investigate (and to see if we were okay.)

They pushed their way in, seeing both Jasper and I were fine.

"It sure is hot in here," Artois from across the street said. He was famous for stating the bloody obvious.

"What is it?" his wife asked, peering into the hole.

"Your guess is as good as mine," I said.

"The cops are here," Jasper said, and he went to let them in.

"Head back to your homes," Officer Marshall demanded, but no one moved.

The fire fighters arrived with hoses at the ready. They followed the heat and sprayed the object from above. Instead of getting cooler, it hissed, and it spat. More steam came out. It was getting hotter, to the point of melting off our clothes.

"Pull back! Pull back!" Officer Marshall demanded. The guys wearing the protective clothing couldn't feel the heat like we could. Within seconds they ceased the water assault.

Just then the insurance company representative arrived, "Whoa!" he said.

That was the last thing I heard.

***

I came to in bed with the covers pulled up to my neck, certain I'd just had a bad dream about a green thing plummeting through the ceiling. I went out to investigate.

In the living room what I saw was a giant scooping apparatus which was being lowered into the hole with the intention of lifting the green crater out of my house. It sounded like a good plan.

The mouth of the thing opened, large, larger, then as large as it could go. It went under the thing with its jaws at the ready and clamped down.

"All systems go!" someone shouted.

The apparatus twisted and creaked. It sang out then gave in with a sigh and a broken jaw. Metal teeth were bent and twisted as what remained attached to the lifting apparatus was pulled back up.

"Now what?" I asked.

"Ma'am," Officer Marshall said, "why don't you and your son book into a hotel for a few days? You might even have insurance to cover it."

"Act of God," I said.

"My brother-in-law is an insurance guy, and I asked him about it. He said most policies cover meteors, so if we can determine if this thing is a meteor, then everything will be covered."

"And who decides what it is, or isn't?"

"We've contacted someone who might be able to advise us or point us in the right direction."

I sat down in my favorite chair — without exception my little piece of peace in chaos.

***

When no one was looking, I went downstairs to take a closer look at the thing. As I drew nearer there seemed to be a sound, humming, or buzzing getting stronger the closer I got in addition to the increase of heat. There was also a smell which made me put my hand over my nose.

Standing beside it, a feeling came over me like everything had turned upside down. In fact, when I looked up, the guests who were standing in the living room were mirrored below like their body was on the top floor and their shadow downstairs floating through the floor with me. It was a strange feeling, like I was down there but not alone.

The shadow-like things were mirrored images with green lights, energy leading to the object. I studied the guests upstairs and their counterpart down; when they moved their shadow-like energy moved too.

I walked around one of the rays and nearer to the fallen mass and the heat lessened. If I followed the pattern using the shadow energies, I could get closer to the fallen object.

Examining it more closely, I was drawn to slits on the surface of the thing. They were shaped like eyes, but there wasn't a pupil, eyelid nor eyelashes. After circling it I felt dizzy.

To steady myself, I leaned my arm on the wall. Next thing I knew the wall had shifted and I was outside my house. The wall of my basement had become a turnstile.

Other than the grass, nothing back looked like it ought to. The shed was gone and so was the bicycle rack and my son's bike. Another thing, the neighbor's houses were all gone.

I began walking, wishing I had a rope attached to the house to hang onto in case I got lost,

I looked up and there was no sun and no sky. What had replaced them was just green above and all around, except for the trees. The trees were branchless, mere trunks reaching skyward.

I pinched myself, to make sure I was awake. I was.

I turned around and observed my house. The encroaching object was visible, half in and half out.

For a moment, I wanted to turn back until a feeling came over me. I felt like singing and I did. Tom Jones' *The Green, Green Grass of Home.*

Swaying and dancing with myself, it was like I was floating in a cloud. Then a hand was in mind, my husband Luther's hand.

I threw my arms around his neck, and he did the same around mine.

We kissed, and we danced.

When the song ended, he bowed, blew me a kiss, and disappeared.

I wiped a tear away.

***

Feeling more alone now than on the day he died, I wrapped my arms around myself and moved toward the house.

Back inside again, I was drawn to the object which seemed to be shifting and humming. Something else, it was turning anti-clockwise.

Upstairs I heard a scream followed by a crash. A body fell through the hole, joined with its shadow energy then came to rest of the surface of the object. The man's flesh sizzled and spit, until all that remained was an X-shape where the man's arms and legs had splayed.

My stomach lurched as I made my way upstairs.

***

The blank faces said it all.

I went to Jasper and asked who the man was. He explained it was a camera man from the local newspaper. He'd tried to get the best shot but leaned in too far.

"Everybody out!" Marshall demanded. This time he wasn't taking no for an answer.

Jasper and I had our home to ourselves again, what was left of it anyway.

***

Officer Marshall and two additional officers were stationed at the front of my house.

Two more officers arrived and were stationed around the back.

They cordoned off the area with tape. Made nosy neighbors cross the street.

Jasper and I pulled back the curtains and peeked out just as a procession of black vehicles screeched to a stop. Doors opened simultaneously like a scene from *Men in Black*. Black suits. Ray-bans.

"Oh dear," Officer Marshall said. "I think the expert we contacted may have brought in the authorities."

"Oh boy, did he ever," I said.

"Whoa," Jasper exclaimed when he clapped eyes on the only woman in the entourage.

She was dressed in a red two-piece suit with a tailored jacket and above the knee skirt. Under the jacket she wore a white blouse with open collar and a necklace with a diamond heart. Topping off the look was a pair of seven-inch red heels and a matching handbag.

The men held back as the woman mounted the stairs.

She was clearly the leader of the pack.

Jasper and I went to the entryway, along-side of Marshall and the two other officers. We formed a half a horseshoe.

The woman showed her identification. She was from Homeland Security, and she had another agent with her. There were two from the F.B.I. Two from the C.I.A. Two from the Department for The Protection of Aliens. Two from Secret Service.

"Where is it?" the woman demanded. Her name was Charlotte Cassidy. She removed her dark sunglasses and her raven hair immediately contrasted with her blue eyes. In her hand, she carried an object which ticked. "It's not as big as I imagined it to be." She approached the hole with the device extended and it fell silent.

"Radiation detector?" Jasper whispered.

I shrugged my shoulders.

The C.I.A. man, Frank Dune, kept putting his sunglasses on and taking them off again even though he was inside. It was very annoying. His partner, Jake Flatts elbowed him and told him to knock it off. "Ma'am, what do you know about this object?"

"It fell through my roof. It's ridiculously hot. It hums, sometimes buzzes. They tried to use a forklift to get it out of here, it broke it." I moved in closer, motioning to explain about the X-shaped form left by the dead guy.

"It's gone," Jasper said.

"What's gone?" Charlotte asked.

Officer Marshall chimed in. "A photographer fell in and melted onto it. There had been an imprint of his body, in the shape of an X, but it is no longer visible."

"Perhaps it was never there?" she said.

"It was absolutely there," I said, "We have plenty of witnesses."

"HOLY MACKERELL!" one of the guys from The Department for The Protection of Aliens (T.D.F.T.P.O.A.) said. His name was Alex Greene, and he was champing at the bit to go down and see it.

Charlotte took the lead, suggesting the group split up. She pointed at who should remain upstairs and who should go downstairs with her. I was included in the latter group.

Alex Greene and his partner Jessie Filtch were clearly miffed at being excluded, but Charlotte thought it best for her and her team to access the danger first before letting the others loose.

***

When I reached the bottom stair, having walked slowly so I could think on the way — sometimes being old has its advantages — I wondered if I should tell them about the dance with my husband. I realized I should, even though it was really none of their business.

I immediately noticed a change in the object. In two of the eye-like slots were two actual eyes. The color wasn't human though, as there were flecks of green in the background and in place of the pupil was something fireball red. I gasped and moved on.

Once I recovered, I expected the guests to be amazed or at least interested in the shadows emanating from the folks upstairs. Oddly enough, they didn't seem to notice.

Charlotte was busy waving her no longer ticking ticker around. She came closer to me. "What exactly worries you about this thing? It seems perfectly harmless to me."

I was saved from saying something I would have regretted by P. G. Willow ('Penguin' for short) — the National Security representative. "Have a bit of sensitivity, will you? This woman's house has been invaded and smashed to bits." He paused, "Have you considered that it might hatch?"

"It's not even in the shape of an egg," Charlotte returned after scoffing.

"An egg as we know it," Penguin retorted.

Charlotte rolled her eyes.

"What worries me, "I said trying not to sound too cross when I felt cross, "is not so much this thing, but all of you tramping through my home. Why are you here anyway? Why aren't the guys from the Department for The Protection of Aliens down here instead of the F.B.I., C.I.A. and Homeland Security?"

"It is very hot," Charlotte's counter man from Homeland Security offered. His name was Brad Hitt, and he was good at stating the bloody obvious like my neighbor had been.

I meandered around, trying to draw attention to the shadows. Walking in and out of them. Nothing.

Was I the only one who could see them?

"What are those gaps in the surface?" Hitt asked.

I moved in and asked him which ones. I wondered what he could see and couldn't see. He said the hundreds or thousands of empty looking slot-like things. Then he reached out and would have touched the thing if I hadn't stopped him in time.

"Are you trying to kill yourself?"

Charlotte chimed in, "I think we have seen enough. The thing needs to be cooled down. Call the fire department. After they cool it down, we can roll it out of here. Easy-peasy."

I told her what happened when the fire department tried that.

Charlotte spoke directly into her phone, "The object in question heats up when water is poured onto it. I repeat, it heats up rather than cools down when chilly water is poured onto it." She crossed the room. We all followed.

"Wait a minute," Hitt said. We all waited. "Never mind," he said.

Charlotte and her entourage left after giving us specific instructions:

#1. No one new is allowed in the house.

#2. No posting anything on social media or anywhere else without her permission.

Then they were gone, except for two.

***

Remaining were Alex Greene and his partner, Jessie Filtch. The two guys from the Department for The Protection of Aliens.

"Mom, can I have a word?"

We excused ourselves and went into my office.

"Mom, I think these two guys are idiots."

"Jasper, what a thing to say."

"I think we should call someone, an expert. Like Sam and Dean on Supernatural. They'd know what to do."

I shook my head. "Uh Jasper, they are fictional characters."

"I know Mom, but there have to be some guys like that in real life."

"Why don't you surf the net and see what you can come up with?"

I left Jasper in my office and went to find Alex and Jessie. They were wearing some weird protective gear including uniforms and masks and with the guns they were carrying, they looked like the Ghostbusters.

I expected to lead the way, but instead followed the boys. They were hauling so much extra stuff, tubes, and gadgets. One of the guys was ticking.

The boys worked together well, with a strange osmosis. One knew what the other was thinking before he communicated. They moved close to the object and wearing protective gloves put their hands upon it. Their suits did the job — at first. They exchanged glances and gave each other a thumb's up.

I moved in a bit closer, detecting an odd smell. Something was burning. First Jessie's glove lit up and then Alex's. They ran over to the sink and tore off their disintegrated gloves with the other hand. Their hands had been burned, but it wasn't as bad as it could have been.

"Whoa!" Jessie said after he'd pulled off his mask. "That son of a bitch is hotter than hell."

This outburst of truth made me laugh as Alex pulled off his mask. "Did you notice the thing?

The two men looked at each other and then at me. I wasn't certain what they were referring to so kept quiet.

"Yeah, Jessie said. "The eyes."

I was surprised they could see them and said so.

"Wait a minute," Alex said. "Are you telling us you can see them without any eye gear?"

I nodded.

"What else can you see?" Jessie asked.

I hesitated and said I'd be right back. They put their hoods back on and I went upstairs to demonstrate the shadow energy. I waited, expecting to hear something from them, like a scream of delight, but heard nothing."

"Oh, you're back," they said.

"Notice anything?"

"May I use your bathroom?" Alex said and upstairs he went.

Jessie put his hood on and when Alex returned they exchanged glances.

"So, you can see the shadows then?"

"We put our hands through it," Jessie admitted. "And we also got a read on it."

I moved in closer. "Well don't keep me in suspense."

"It's an ionized-air glow, Rydberg atoms, hence the green tint," Alex said. "It's difficult to explain as it usually only occurs in space or in places like the aurora borealis. It's extremely rare, I mean it's unheard of in someone's basement."

I had my mouth gaping open. I closed it.

"Aluminum based," Jessie explained. "Not toxic or dangerous. We think the object is here by accident, from far, far away. Given the sheer size and shape of it, not to mention the weight of it, sending it back is not going to be easy. In fact, we probably don't have the technology to do it."

"I need a drink," I said.

As I was making my way upstairs Jessie asked, "What about the wall?"

"Assuming she can see it," Alex said.

Pretending I hadn't heard them, I continued. Then I threw back a shot of whiskey.

"Mom?"

"I'm in the kitchen, love."

"I found two guys, like Sam and Dean. They are driving here now, about forty-five minutes away, using their GPS. I hope you don't mind, but I offered them a running tab. Up to one hundred dollars to cover their expenses."

I smiled. "That's fine."

"They have a website and lots of testimonials and experience in the supernatural, the occult and the alienesque."

"Good going Jasper. You let me know when they arrive. In the mean-time I'll keep the two guests downstairs busy."

"Are you okay, Mom? You look a little tired?"

"I'm tired, but excited about it at the same time.

"Me too!"

***

I returned to the basement, confirming I could see it.

"Have you gone through it? To the other side?" Jessie asked.

"I went over and leaned on the wall like this." I demonstrated and once again went straight through. The boys were already suited up and they followed.

"What's the air like?" Jessie asked.

"It's fresh and beautiful."

They removed their masks.

"When did you first notice the void?" Alex asked.

"I didn't really, I just leaned into it by accident."

"It looks very strange with all of this green sky," Alex said. He touched the grass, said it felt artificial.

They walked in the opposite direction to where I had gone before. I followed closely behind. We walked for quite some time, listening carefully to the quiet. "Why did you boys call it the void?"

"He was just kidding," Jessie said. "The void is what they call something like this in the gaming world or virtual reality. We aren't certain what this is yet, but we feel like this world is the world your object originated from."

"In fact," Alex added. "That thing would be camouflaged here, like a chameleon."

I heard a loud whistle. Interesting to note I could hear sounds from inside my house in this other place. Alex and Jessie did not react to the sound as I made my way back to the entry way and walked straight in. The boys were on my heels, but they did not come through. I reached my hand into the void (for want of a better word) and then pulled it back. It was filled with a jelly-like green substance. I went in again with both hands, reaching desperately for Jessie and Alex. I screamed out their names through the wall and even tried to push myself back through again but had no luck.

Jasper whispered loudly.

"Bring them down here Jasper, I think we need their help — NOW."

***

Our Sam and Dean were two young lads, barely older than Jasper. They were loaded down with equipment as they made their way down the stairs. The tallest of the two had blond hair and was named Bert (short for Albert) and the second youth, who had an army style haircut was named Leo (short for Galileo.)

After we exchanged a few niceties, I explained about the missing agents and the void.

Leo spoke into a microphone he had on his phone. He described the object including size and dimensions. He asked me to explain how the void worked.

Bert walked over to the green object for a closer look. He reached out his hand and touched the object before I could stop him. "It's totally cool," he said. "I mean temperature-wise. Given Jasper's description of it earlier, I'd say something has short-circuited."

I touched it myself; it felt exceptionally smooth and cool. I searched for the pair of eyes, without any luck. I wondered about the shadows and asked Jasper to run up the stairs, so I could check it out. Nothing. Bert and Leo watched me intently.

"I think whoever owns this thing must have a tractor beam on it."

"We should say, HAD a tractor beam on it," Bert said. "Because it seems to have malfunctioned."

"Can I come down now?" Jasper asked.

I apologized for forgetting about him.

"The guys on the other side, what are their names?" Leo asked.

We called out to them. Nothing.

"So, the tractor beam thing," I said, "It stopped working, so how do we fix it? And if we fix it, will they be able to reel it back in again?"

"If we could get the void to open, then push the object through," Leo said.

"And get the guys back," Jasper added.

I'd still have a massive hole in my roof, but at least then I could get it fixed.

Together the four of us stood on one side of the object. "On the count of three," Bert said, and we pushed it with everything we had.

"It was a clever idea," Bert said when we couldn't shift it one iota. He hesitated for a moment and then asked, "When you were on the other side, did you sense any danger?"

I thought about it. I hadn't and said so. "One thing," I admitted. "Jasper, this will come as a shock to you. I had hoped to tell you in private."

I explained about dancing with my husband. Worried, I asked Jasper how he felt about it. He said he just wished he had been there with me.

"Did he ask about me?"

I wished he had but he hadn't. It all happened so fast.

"Let me get this one thing straight," Alex interrupted. "It wasn't your husband. It was a manifestation of your husband. Supernatural beings can read minds; some can conjure spirits and even replicate the living."

"But he felt real, even smelled real."

"That's exactly what they want you to think," Leo said.

Outside I heard car tires come to a screeching halt.

"They're back," I said as we made our way toward the front door.

"Damn it," Leo and Bert said. "We have a right to be here. We aren't going anywhere."

I opened the door.

We stood firmly in place with a powerful sense of purpose and determination that we would not be moved.

* * *

Leading the pack this time was not Charlotte. Instead, it was the President.

He was taller than everyone else, dressed in a thick overcoat which was accentuated with a pair of leather gloves. His bodyguards kept close, speaking into microphones, and packing visible heat.

"Mr. President," I said with a curtsey. He extended his ungloved hand. I introduced him to Jasper, then Bert and Leo. "Welcome to my home, Mr. President."

He bowed his head and came inside and asked, "So, where did they go through?"

How did he know? Had they bugged my house? I was annoyed and said so.

Charlotte came forward with her phone extended, pushed play. On her phone was a message from Jessie and Alex.

"Holy cow!" Bert exclaimed.

"Why didn't we think of that?" Leo asked.

"You wouldn't now, would you?" Charlotte said with an unbecoming arrogance which the President's raised eyebrows indicated he wasn't pleased about.

"Follow me," I said and led them into the basement.

"Wait a minute," the President said. "How come this thing isn't giving off heat anymore?" He turned to Charlotte. "I thought you said it was red-hot."

Charlotte realized the President was right and asked for an update.

"It seems to have happened when the guys went into the void," I offered.

"Call them again," the President ordered, Charlotte tried, but they didn't answer.

Bert said to the President, "We were just considering the possibility of rolling the thing out of here now that it's cool. If we can open the void and get the boys in and it out, it could be considered as an exchange of good will."

"To whom?" the President asked.

"To whoever sent it here," Leo said.

"Please tell me more," the President said and soon Charlotte and her entourage were gathered around listening too.

"We think," Leo said, "that whoever this thing belongs to must have had a tractor beam on it. We think the tractor beam malfunctioned — but in either case, we need to get those two guys out before it turns back on again."

The President shook Leo's and Bert's hand. He turned to Charlotte. "Hire these two."

The boys were flattered but declined his offer, then explained their past experiences with the supernatural, the occult and the alienesque. They told the President about their five million plus hits on YouTube and millions of followers on Social Media.

"Well now, that's very impressive," the President said. His hand slipped into his pocket, and he pulled out two business cards and gave them to the boys. They in turn, gave him their business cards.

"Now let's get to the matter at hand," the President said. "How to get our guys back and pronto."

I leaned against the wall, like I had done before and hoped to go through but this time it didn't work.

* * *

We managed to move the green object ever so slightly, so it was in position if the void opened.

"All we can do now is wait," the President said. Then he called Charlotte over, thanked us for being outstanding citizens, and then made a motion to depart.

"Can I ask a favor?" Bert said.

"Sure thing," the President said.

"Can we take a selfie for our website?"

The President said, 'No problem' and they did several.

We went upstairs and waited for a sign. Any sign.

***

Day turned into night.

Outside the wind was whistling and rattling the roof tiles like it was running a race against itself. I closed my eyes, shivered, looked and up through the gap in the ceiling and spotted a ray of light in the starry, starry night.

I gasped and soon everyone was standing near me and looking up.

"Whoa!" Leo exclaimed. "I think it's the tractor beam."

"Talk about beam me up Scotty!" Bert said.

The tractor beam came down, snaked through the hole, down into the basement where it latched onto the green object. The tractor beam was also green, but it shimmered and shook as it reached out and took hold of the thing.

Once it had a firm grip, it seemed to stop, then rev-up the engines. The sound was deafening, and we all covered our ears, as it lifted the object away from the wall first and then slowly but steadily skyward.

We couldn't take our eyes off it. We could have been in danger — still we could not look away. It rose higher and higher and into the night sky. We went outside, to see more of what was at the other end, but from all perspectives nothing was visible except for the beam of a green line which was carrying the object away.

Once it was completely gone, so high up it was invisible to the naked eye, we remained together standing silently until I said, "Okay, the object is gone, but what are we going to do about Alex and Jessie? They are still trapped in the void."

"Guess we need a Plan B," Leo said.

"We'll leave that to you," Charlotte said as she pushed the speed dial on her phone and filled the President in and then declared the case closed. "There are no security issues here, and no aliens." She and her entourage packed up and headed for their vehicles.

"Wait a minute!" I shouted. "Don't you even care about your men?"

"Collateral damage," Charlotte said as she slammed the door of her car. They drove away.

"I guess it's up to us," I said.

Bert and Leo looked at each other.

Bert said, "I'm sorry, but we don't know what to do or how to get them back. We're going to head off too, get some shut eye. We'll call you in the morning if we think of anything."

Jasper and I were not amused. Now that the object was gone, everyone was leaving. Abandoning us.

Jasper went to his room, and I got into my pajamas, constantly thinking about the missing men. I tried to distract myself by reading a mystery novel, but the mystery right under my own roof demanded my attention. After two hours of tossing and turning I got up to make myself a cup of tea.

I'd have put on my housecoat if I had known that company was coming.

***

Sipping tea, wondering how I could resolve the dilemma I gazed up at the stars, as a tear trickled down my cheek. Two men were lost somewhere in the void, family-less, friend-less, country-less. They'd been brave citizens. They deserved better.

I grabbed a chocolate biscuit and was about to take a bite when I noticed a shimmering green star. A green star? I rubbed my eyes, but it was still there, winking at me. I went outside, to get a full view of the night sky.

It wasn't a star.

It was moving, falling fast in my direction, growing bigger and bigger.

"Oh no!" I cried out to no one. Then I called for Jasper, and he came out running. I pointed up, while contemplating a quick move if we needed to get out of its way.

As the gap between them and us lessened we couldn't contain our excitement and jumped for joy as the thing halted and there they were.

Two black umbrellas popped open, Alex and Jessie each grabbed a hold of one and their descent toward us began.

Wearing suits made of a reflective material Alex and Jessie fell gently toward us.

After landing smoothly, the pair reached inside of their suits and pulled out two green bottles. After flipping the top open they downed the contents. They climbed out of their suits revealing the clothes in which they had departed. They slipped the bottles back inside and attached them to the umbrellas.

The tractor beam latched onto the umbrellas and suits. We waved as the objects were pulled skyward and watched until we could see them no more.

"Welcome back!" Jasper and I exclaimed.

"I could murder a cup of tea!" Alex said.

"I'd prefer a shot of whiskey," Jessie said.

"Who were they?" I asked. "Or should I say WHAT were they?"

"All in suitable time," our two returned heroes said in unison. "But first we must have biscuits and beverages."

They adjusted to being back, while I plated up. We sat together at the dinner table, sipping. Waiting. They didn't have anything to say. No questions for us, even though the massive green object was no longer in my home.

My patience began to run thin, so I asked them to tell us what happened.

"It was a short holiday," Alex said.

"Yes, a paid vacation," Jessie said.

I stood up. "What do you mean? Where were you? Who had you? Were you imprisoned? What were they like? How did you convince them to send you back?" I sat down again.

Jasper continued, "And what was that green thing? Why was it here? Did someone get their asses kicked for dropping it?"

The men looked at each other with blank faces. They had no idea about what we were talking. Talk about clueless.

"Mom, I think the aliens wiped their minds."

"Agreed. Talk about a clean slate."

There was nothing else we could say or do, other than go to sleep. Jessie bunked down on the sofa, Alex on the La-Z-Boy chair.

Alex jumped up. "Oh, before I forget."

Jessie jumped too. "Yes, we have something for you."

Jasper and I looked at each other, it was like they had been prodded or shocked.

Jessie pulled out of his pocket a green shimmering case. It rippled when I took it into my hand and felt very cool. I opened it and gasped. Inside was my husband's St. Christopher's Medal. The one I had given him on our first wedding anniversary.

Alex handed a similar object to Jasper. Inside was his father's watch. Jasper put it straight onto his wrist. "Did he say anything about me?"

Alex said, "He sees you every single day, both of you. It's true what they say, those who we love are never far away from us."

Both Alex and Jessie jumped this time in unison. "We have to go."

"What now?" I asked. "Are you guys all right?"

"Yes," they said together. "We have something to deliver to the President. Now."

A car pulled up outside and off they went.

***

"We have to deliver it to him ourselves," Jessie and Alex demanded.

It was in the middle of the night, but the President agreed to see them.

When they entered The Oval Office, the President was seated and wearing his silk bathrobe.

"What do you two have for me?" the President asked.

Together Jessie and Alex presented the object to him. It was an exceptionally large green button. On it were the following words, "PUSH ME. JUST DO IT."

"What will happen?" the President asked.

"We don't know."

"I need to ask someone, one of my advisers. I can't just..."

"But you're the President," Jessie said.

"Yeah, you can do anything, can't you?"

The President put the green button on his desk next to the red button. Together they looked quite Christmassy.

Jessie and Alex said, "Outside. Outside. Outside."

"Okay boys, okay," the President said. "Let's go."

Once outside the President could not wait to push it and he did.

The sky turned from blue to green as a tractor beam covered the country from coast to coast, pulling up every single AR-15.

EPILOGUE

Far, far away, on the planet with the green sky and green earth but where the trees were nothing but trunks, the aliens repurposed the earthly materials they had gathered.

The AR-15s were fashioned into branches.

The bottles were hung from the branches, and they whistled in the wind.

The umbrellas provided rain and sun protection.

Whenever the aliens needed more AR-15s, they lit up the button, and the Presidents always pushed it.

DARRYL AND ME

O N THE SAME DAY *I found out I was pregnant, my husband died.*

I am in a war zone. I am not alone. My baby is with me, inside me.

I cross my arms over my baby, protecting the child as I walk down the street as bombs explode around us. I try to find shelter for us, but the bombs are getting closer and closer.

I am lost, but unafraid. My child kicks my hand for reassurance. We are bonding together while the rest of the world blows apart.

I stop and look at myself in a mirror in the center of the street. I am wearing a bright red dress with matching red shoes and black stockings. I finger fluff my hair, reach into my handbag for some lippy. I make a kiss imprint on the glass then throw my head back and take a selfie. I post it on Instagram. Or try to. Not sure if I have enough bars.

I hear a siren screaming. Coming in my direction. It is heading toward the mirror. I reach out to grab it, but a hand grabs mine. I scream. The siren screams.

"Get inside. Are you mad? Get in!" the ambulance driver says in a language I do not know or understand. Thankfully, there are subtitles.

I hesitate before climbing in. I need to find Darryl. Darryl is here somewhere, and our baby needs his or her father. Darryl is looking for me, and we are looking for him. Our child is the magnet. The radar. The GPS.

I throw back my head, and I cry his name loud and clear, "Darryl!" I listen and then cry out again. I call his name and listen. The ambulance driver says I am crazy and throws his car into reverse.

The ambulance hits the mirror and a bomb goes off. Bits fly everywhere.

There is an awful lot of blood on pieces of glass.

I wake up and I scream.

***

I had the same dream every night after Darryl died. I kept reliving how it happened, even though I wasn't there. It was a routine operation as a part of the United Nations Peace Keeping Force.

It is a coping mechanism, this dreaming it, living it. Trying to find the man I love when we buried him. The funeral was beautiful. I was so proud of Darryl. He gave up his life for the cause and I get it. I admire him for his dedication because it made him a better man.

They draped the flag over his casket. I tossed two handfuls of dirt into the ground then fell to my knees sobbing. My mother and others including my friends tried to help, but I screamed them away. I wanted to be alone with Darryl. I wanted to tell him about the baby.

Our baby.

I was not leaving until I had the chance to say goodbye. I lie down beside the open grave on my stomach, resting my head on my arms. I told him how much I loved him and said goodbye before I blew him a kiss and rose to my feet.

Mom was at my side and so was Moni then. Each took one of my arms, pulled me back together again. We made our way to the car.

On the way home, I felt Darryl's presence. His arms wrapped around me. The hair rose on my forearms, I could smell him. I could feel him.

Then, he was gone.

At home inside the door, an oblong-shaped box was waiting for me with a bow across it's middle. I wanted to ask what it was doing there, but the grief in the room swept me away. I floated from person to person, taking on their 'I'm so sorry,' and 'it will get better in time' clichés. The usual after funeral bullshit.

After they went, I felt empty.

Mom tucked me into bed, like she used to do when I was a little girl.

After she closed the door behind her, I raised my clenched fists up to the heavens for taking Darryl.

Then I fell to my knees in gratitude for our baby growing inside of me.

***

I wake up staring at the empty space beside me, wiping away the drool from the corners of my mouth. The doorbell is ringing. I throw back the covers and step onto the floor. Before I can even make it out of our room, my room mother flies at me with her arms open wide.

I need to ask her for that key back.

"I was so worried," she says, hugging, squeezing, and making me feel like a little girl once again. She steps back and looks at my face.

I push my hair behind my left ear and try to smile. I point myself in the direction of the kitchen and, when I get there, I fill the coffee pot with water. I open the dishwasher to keep myself busy while the coffee machine spits behind me. Mother closes the dishwasher door, pushes the necessary buttons, and backs me into a chair where she gives me no alternative but to sit.

She is in Darryl's seat, and I am in no one's seat. When she realizes, she moves into the other no one's chair. She jumps up before I can and pours the coffee. I add cream and sugar to mine and I sip. One sip is enough. I run to the bathroom. I forgot coffee triggered morning sickness for a few of my friends.

When I return to the kitchen, mother has made a cup of decaffeinated chamomile tea. It is meant to calm me down.

I sit and sip the bitter, hot drink, and watch as mother moves about in my kitchen like a person on a mission. "I am making you some toast," she says as it pops up almost on cue. Mother uses the knife to mush down the crusts, another flashback to when I was a little girl. She then spreads on the butter and turns around to look at me.

Mom adds some strawberry jam and goes into the fridge. She pulls out the block of cheese that she shreds over my toast. She places it back on top of the toaster (with the jam and cheese side facing up.) She pushes the button down to let the toast heat up for a few seconds.

This is another ritual from my childhood, and I am grateful she is here.

Mom cuts the toast into triangles, and I cannot believe how wonderful it tastes when I bite into it. I eat both slices, and then sip some more tea as it doesn't taste as bitter now since she put in a few squirts of honey. She thinks I didn't notice.. I take mom's hand and tell her thank you once again.

Baby is no longer hungry.

Baby's mother is no longer comfortably numb.

Baby's grandmother is no longer feeling useless.

Mother cleans up, prattling on about this and that. I listen without appreciating her efforts to distract. I allow her to think it is working, her distraction tactics. To be honest, I cannot keep up with her line of thought and her pace. It feels like I am listening to her from under water.

She laughs. I jump. I am back from wherever my mind travelled to. I went somewhere in a flash. I felt myself go.

I was a little girl, hiding under the stairs. Then I went up the stairs and into the closet where it was very dark. The sleeves from my father's shirt moved. I ran out, giving my hiding spot away. I got caught.

"I remember the time," mother says, bringing me back to the present. It is like she is telling the story for the first time. "You used to hide the crusts when you were a little girl. Before I started crushing them with a knife, we would find them in pockets, in planters. Ah, the ones in planters. Those would sop up the water, killing some of the plants before we figured out what you were doing."

"Killing the plants," I mimic.

She comes to me, kneels, and asks, "Are you all right, love?"

I almost laugh at her ridiculous question, but catch myself before I do, before I say, "NO I AM FUCKING NOT ALL RIGHT." Darryl. Jesus Darryl. I push the chair back, creating space between mother and I and stand up. I am like a zombie. I do not need to feed on human flesh though. I want Darryl. I smile when I repeat need to feed need to feed need to feed again in my head.

Now that I am standing, I should be moving. My feet want to be going somewhere, anywhere, and yet I find myself doing the exact opposite. I sit back down again. Mother does the same. She sips her cup of coffee, probably freezing cold by now.

I stand up and say, "I'm tired," even though I just woke up, I know this. She knows this. Yet I do not fucking care. I walk back to our room, my room, mother following behind. When she catches up, she places her right hand on my hip like she needs to guide me. Like I could get lost on the way.

At the door now, I turn and face her. She has tears in her eyes, but they are not spilling over. She knows how it feels to lose a husband because she lost daddy, but it is not the same thing. They had a whole life together. They had each other for thirty-seven years before daddy died. We were only married for two and a half years. Darryl will never see his son or daughter. I want to say this, but I do not.

I think she knows what I am thinking, although I do not know for certain. It's that mother-daughter osmosis thing. She kisses me on the forehead as she tucks me into bed. She goes out and closes the door behind her.

I get out of bed again, go to the mirror, and look at myself. In forty-eight hours, I have aged ten years. Although I have been sleeping for most of it, the bags under my eyes are huge. It looks like I have been crying the entire time, but the truth is, I am out of tears already. My face no longer looks like me. I am a stranger, even to myself.

I run a little water and splash it onto my face before soaking warm water into a face cloth, Darryl's. I hold it over myself to breathe him in.

I find his bath towel, strip off my clothing, and wrap it around me. It envelops me and warms me like I am in his arms. I sit like this for what seems like forever. Like he's holding me. No tears flow. There are no tears left to cry. It's like Darryl is wrapping around us. Holding us together, the three of us, Darryl, the baby, and me.

Mother's knocking on the door pulls me back to the present. I must have dropped off to sleep. I stand up too fast when the door flies open. Darryl's towel hits the floor.

Mother and the neighbour walk into the room, and I grab Darryl's towel in time and hide my nakedness. I begin to giggle and cannot stop.

Mother and looks worried. The neighbor's eyes are bulging right out of her head. Soon, they will be calling the men in the white fitted jackets to come and collect me if I do not pull myself together.

***

It is my wedding day, and I am walking down the aisle on my dad's arm in a grand church. I know I am dreaming because dad never walked me down the aisle. He was already dead when Darryl and I got married, and Darryl and

I did not get married in a church. Elton John's, "Your Song," is our song. I mean, it was Darryl's and my song. We actually preferred the Ewan McGregor version since we loved Moulin Rouge.

Dad and I greet those we see along the way. Grandma Eleanor, who has been dead since I was a little girl, blows me a kiss. I take a flower out of my bouquet. Baby's breath, her favourite. I give it to her.

She smiles, and a tear falls down her cheek.

Across the aisle, there is my cousin, Ruth. She and I were remarkably close when we were children. Now, we rarely see each other. I expect she is thinking the exact same thing as I am as I pass her by. Note to myself: ask her over for dinner sometime soon.

There are Darryl's two younger brothers, Dale, and Donny. Their parents had a kind of thing about the letter D. Note to myself: do not continue with said tradition.

I see my other grandma, my mom's mom. She did not make it to our wedding. She and mother are holding hands, and I unhook myself from dad for a few seconds to go and give them both a big hug. My knees buckle a bit when Grandma reaches out, takes my hand into hers, and drops something into it. I instinctively close my fingers around it; even though I do not see what it is, I can feel that it is a key. Dad pulls my arm into his and we get back on track making our way down the aisle.

My bridesmaids, Trish, and Moni (short for Monique) are close to me now. They look stunning in their antique white dresses, but wait, I was the one who wore antique white.

Dad turns me, removes my hand from his arm, and wraps it around Darryl's. I turn to look at my husband to be, but it is not Darryl. Well, it once was Darryl, but now it is not anymore. He is dead. He is a rotting corpse.

I scream as the green slime pours out of his lips when he tries to smile. I'm not the only one screaming.

Everyone is screaming.

Everything is screaming–even the machines.

I open my hand.

I swallow the key.

Bits of glass shatter everywhere.

***

I open my eyes. I am not at home, but in the hospital. I hear ticking, heart beats. Beeping. Whispering. I close my eyes again. I pretend to be asleep.

"No change."

"Can't give up."

"What about the baby?"

The baby. Those two words bring me back to reality and I attempt to sit up and discover I'm unable to.

When I cannot move my arms or legs, I scream. I clutch at my stomach, my baby, our little one, and discover the baby bump is bigger now. How long have I been sleeping?

"Mom?"

"Oh, darling! Darling," she says. "You are going to be fine," she coos but I do not believe her. Not a single word.

"How long have I been here?" I ask, and my head is like an echo chamber as the words reverberate inside my skull.

She hugs me and holds me instead of answering. When I pull away, she holds my head in her hand and gazes into my eyes like she's trying to find me.

I try not to blink but I cannot stop. Don't you hate it when that happens? As soon as you try not to do something, your body betrays you and makes you do it even more.

She says nothing. She thinks I cannot handle the truth. The handle the truth voice in my head is Jack Nicholson's in *A Few Good Men.* Darryl loved that movie. We watched it so many times I lost count.

"I want to know," I hear myself saying, but the way she is looking at me, I am uncertain if I said it out loud or in my head. I try again, this time a little louder and she reacts.

"Let me," she says and then she leaves, returning in a few moments with someone I do not recognize. The two of them move around the room like they are blocking out a stage for a play in the theatre. They whisper, then look at me, and whisper more.

How rude.

I wait, like I'm invisible and try not to explode.

The stranger sticks a needle in my arm and off I go thinking hospital staff in street clothes should be outlawed.

I dream again that I am walking down the street, looking for Darryl while the bombs go off.

***

The bump on me is even bigger now. In fact, noticeably larger. When the baby moves, I see bits of him or her through my skin. Limbs which make imprints like turning me inside out as our child pushes against the walls of my stomach.

I am no longer at the hospital. I am at home, seated in a nursery, rocking in a nursing chair which doesn't rock in the usual sense of the word. Instead, it glides.

Sleeping sheep with zzzs surrounding their heads line the walls waiting to be counted. I begin counting, then smile, looking at the crib. Time stands still, it has to, because nothing is happening here, today, now.

I raise myself out of the chair, half awake and half asleep. I touch the mobile and it begins to chime out Frere Jacques. I sing along, as I pick up a blanket with a sheep on it.

I fold the blanket smaller and smaller, until it is a tiny square. Then, I place it back in the crib and catch a glimpse of myself in the mirror in the corner.

Part of the mirror is visible and part of it is not because a something is covering it. I move closer, lifting off the dust shield to reveal a treasure that has been in my family for decades. A family heirloom handed down from my mother's mother's mother's mother.

The frame is cool to the touch as I run my fingers along it. It is wooden and engraved with pairs of entwined hands. The laced finger imprints feel even cooler to the touch. I move my body closer until my baby bump pushes against the glass. It does not touch it. It goes through it. As I push nearer and nearer, my baby bump disappears into it.

I take a step back and my baby bump disconnects with a sucking sound. My baby kicks and kicks again as I move away from the mirror and return to the chair in which I had begun. As I sit, the mobile restarts and we begin to glide in tune with it.

My baby settles, and we sleep.

***

"Wake up Cath," Darryl says.

I roll toward him and snuggle into him. The baby bumps between us. We cannot get as close to each other as we used to do, but we are closer on many other levels.

The alarm goes off and I am hugging onto Darryl's pillow, not him. My baby kicks and I get out of bed to wander down along the corridor, semi awake to the bathroom where I go to the loo. I turn on the water, stand in the shower, and let the water run over me.

My baby loves the water, and we remain there until the hot water runs out and turns into cold. Hungry now, I throw on my housecoat and head downstairs as mom walks in through the front door. She must have rung the bell when I was in the shower. Note to myself: ask Mom to give back the key.

"I brought gifts," she says. She dumps an entire box of iced donuts onto the table; the donuts still warm and smelling like heaven. I stuff one into my mouth and she one into hers. We hug each other and have a second donut before we decide to make a pot of tea.

My baby kicks out a thank you and mom feels it herself. "Oh," I say, as the baby makes its presence further known by doing what feels like a somersault inside of me.

"Are you okay?" Mom asks.

"He's happy," I say.

Mom picks up on the fact that I said he. She doesn't mention it. Instead, she tells me the latest gossip.

I listen out of politeness, not because I am interested in the local goings-on. Before, I mean before I met Darryl, I contributed by jumping on the gossip train. Sometimes, I'd even be the conductor minus the hat. Sometimes, I would be the caboose. One way or the other, I was always on the train. I let the gossip mongers choo-choo me along.

"Have you seen the nursery?" I ask from out of nowhere, while she is in mid-gossip-sentence.

She looks at me like I am a stranger. "Are you sure you are okay?" she asks, with a big frown lining her forehead in the shape of a horizontal question mark.

I realize I have said something weird, perhaps even stupid. I do not know what it is. "I'm fine," I say, trying to reassure her that I am.

I stand up, hoping she will do the same, but she does not. Instead, she removes another donut from the box and takes a bite.

My baby kicks me hard. Like he wants another donut. I have to pee and say so. Mom follows me down the corridor.

"I will meet you in the nursery," I say.

"Okay," Mom replies.

When I join her in the nursery, mom is standing in front of the mirror. I join her, standing at her side and step closer and closer to the glass. I'm testing to see if the baby will go through, like it did yesterday, but it does not. No ripple. No connection. Was I dreaming?

As I turn away, the mobile begins playing Frere Jacques all by itself.

"I rewound it, Cath," she says, "we did a wonderful job decorating, didn't we? I'm so pleased."

I do not remember decorating and don't want to admit it. How could I have forgotten such a thing?

"Your great-great-great-grandmother would be so pleased. I'm happy the mirror belongs to you now."

The world begins to spin and fade. I move forward and almost topple over. Mom catches me, and folder me into the chair where I glide back and forth back and forth.

"Isn't the mirror rightly yours?" I ask.

"Yes, but I don't mind. It's perfect in this room."

Thinking about the mirror, I drift off to sleep. Mother has gone. It is dark in here, except for a light flickering in the corner a little distance away from the mirror.

The baby kicks. He is restless. I stand and walk toward the mirror. As we draw closer, the light brightens. My baby kicks and shifts. I draw the blanket off and look at my baby bump reflection, moving closer and closer. The baby kicks a field goal.

My baby bump bumps against the mirror. Baby kicks again, closing up the gap between the bump and the glass. When the two connect, my baby bump disappears into it. There is a pull, drawing us in.

I am now standing nose to glass. I press myself further in until my full face is inside. My head follows. My baby rolls away into the reflection.

A strong gust of wind picks up somewhere behind us and pushes us in further. Now enough of me is inside to notice the difference in the air. Autumn. Leaves. It was spring where we were and autumn here. How could that be?

I could smell and feel the cool air, whipping around us, welcoming us. A breeze whispers across my skin like a touch.

My baby pushes forwards and back, seeking comfort on the other side. Comfort inside the glass world. I caress my baby bump for reassurance, and my baby pushes back to do the same for me.

It is magnificent there. I am in the middle of a forest. No, I am on a beach with sand, pure white sand and waves crashing and crashing upon the shore.

No, I am near mountains, tall mountains with paths winding around them. It is many worlds all rolled in together. I hear birds singing. There are ravens, crows, blue jays, flamingos, kookaburras, whinchats, sparrows, mockingbirds, and seagulls. I can taste the salt of the ocean on my tongue.

I call out, "Hello," and my voice echoes around and around and around. My baby dances to the echo, tickling, making me giggle. I feel peace, pure and sweet. Joyous. Home.

On the other side, behind me, something pulls me back. I do not want to go. My baby does not want to go, but something grabs me. It rips us out of there. Back.

"What the hell are you doing?" someone shouts. Their voice is wobbly, warbled.

I hear the words, but the voice sounds like it is inside of a cloud.

***

The minute we are back, we want to leave again. We want to be there, to exist there. Only there and nowhere else.

It is Moni and she is very cross at me. "What were you thinking?"

I say nothing as I glance back at the mirror.

"Don't play innocent with me," Moni says. "You were travelling. I mean in another dimension, weren't you?"

"Travelling?" I mimic. I think about it for a second, how crazy I must've looked and said, "I was looking at my reflection, our reflection. The baby and me."

"Most of you was gone!" Moni screams. "GONE!"

I laugh, trying to pretend she had not seen what she had seen. Trying to make her feel like she was crazy. Instead of me. I had been there. I had seen another world. I cross the room, away from the mirror, turn back and walk to the mirror. I make a fist and put it right against the glass, hoping nothing would happen and it didn't.

Moni follows me and does the same thing. Then, we stand face to face and burst into laughter. We must have looked crazy. Insane. Ridiculous.

The baby kicks.

Before long, we are downstairs. Moni says my mom had to leave and that is why she came over.

"I don't need babysitting."

"It has been six months," Moni says, "since Darryl died, and we're all worried about you and the baby."

"The baby and I are doing fine," I say. "I--we still miss him every day, but it is getting easier." It was a lie.

"I know what we should do tomorrow," Moni says. "Let's go to the beach."

It sounds fun and so I agree. I have no plans to wear a bathing suit though.

***

We arrive at the beach with a picnic basket filled with lunch and all kinds of goodies. We kick off our shoes and let the sand squish between our toes even though it's far from warm out.

"Darryl and I used to love coming here in the summertime."

"He is with us here now and always," Moni says.

Moni is right, but it does not stop me from missing him. I want more than his memories. I want him here with his arms around me.

"I miss his arms, his holding me, his breath. I miss everything about him every single day."

Moni puts her arm around my shoulder.

"The hardest part is," I continue, "Darryl will never know our baby and our baby will never know Darryl."

"You don't know what the future holds for you," Moni says.

I know where she is going with this. She is suggesting that I meet someone else. The thought is not worth consideration. I was carrying Darryl's baby for Christ's sake.

"I don't want anyone else. No one could ever replace Darryl or what we had together. Besides, my heart is too broken. I will never love anyone else. My heart belongs to Darryl and Darryl only."

"Don't say that. You do not know what the future might hold for you. Love can happen more than once. Look at my mom. I mean, Dad died, she married my stepdad and found love the second time around. It is not the same. It can never be the same as your first love, but it can still be love. It can be enough. You have to be open to it. They are happy and so could you be in time," Moni says.

I break into a sprint then, as much as an eight-month pregnant woman can sprint and I walk into the water. The temperature is cold but refreshing, and I like the feel of the coolness on my skin.

Moni pushes in beside me.

"This baby loves water."

Moni puts her hand on my belly and the baby kicks. "He sure does," she says.

We stand in the water up to our knees and let the waves wash over us. The baby loves it and does a few somersaults.

"Are you going to tell me about it?" Moni asks.

"I'm not sure what you mean," I say.

"I mean about the mirror thing, what you were doing? Were you travelling? World hopping?"

I think about it and decide she is right. I mean, through the mirror, my baby and I had sort of travelled to another place. Another dimension. The music from *The Twilight Zone* resonates in my head.

"And what would you know about it?" I ask.

"I watch movies, read books. There's even travelling in Alice In Wonderland When I walked in, most of you was gone and it was obvious it was in the mirror. You were in the mirror. So, what did you see? Or did you see anything?"

"I'm not sure I want to talk about it," I say because it is a secret. I want to hold it close to my chest for now. It feels like if I admit it out loud, it might go away. I knew that sounded silly, but it had all been so strange and it had only happened to me once. Twice for the baby, but once for me. I want to be there and to do it again before I speak about it to anyone else.

"Promise me one thing," Moni says as we watch the sun go down on our drive home. "Promise me you won't go in alone. I mean, without someone on this side to pull you back."

I nod in a sort of promise, but I am not sure I intend to keep it.

"I would like to stay at your place tonight, to keep you company," Moni says.

I say it is fine because I am too tired to do anything more than sleep, exhausted from the fresh sea air. My baby is not even moving around inside me.

I get into my pajamas and fall asleep straight away. I dream of Darryl, searching for him, looking high, low, and everywhere. I walk and walk and my feet blister and bleed, but still no Darryl. On occasion, I run into someone or something like a scarecrow in a field. I ask if he has seen Darryl and like in The Wizard of Oz, he points in all directions. Great help he is.

I also ask a weird, beardy woman who works in a circus if she has seen Darryl. She laughs and laughs and laughs.

He is nowhere, so I wake myself up and power up my laptop. I spend the evening looking at photographs of us. Of our life.

When we were together, you could see love all around us. I know it sounds like a stupid cliché, but it was there, especially when Darryl looked at me or when I looked at him. We loved each other with a love that would never again be in a world where we were apart.

As I search through the past alone, I feel like he and the baby and I are together looking at the photographs. The baby is on my lap. Darryl is behind me, looking over my shoulder as I flip from page to page.

The sun is coming up and bringing in a new day when I finish.

Exhausted I go back to bed.

***

"Cath. Cath! CATH!"

What the? Stop it. I want to keep on dreaming.

"CATH!!"

I realize I am hearing Darryl's voice. What? I shake myself awake. I listen and hear it again.

"Cath."

"Darryl?"

I throw back the covers and open the bedroom door. Now that I have answered, he whispers my name again and again.

I find myself in the baby's room where I stand still and listen. I shiver as if a breeze has blown through me. Then I grab the blanket out of the crib and wrap it around my shoulders. The baby is quiet, like he has not awoken yet.

"Cath."

I look at the window. The wind makes it click and clack, then pushes it right open. The cool autumn puts its arms around me, holding me while at the same time pushing me.

"Cath."

I turn toward where the voice is coming from. The mirror. My baby awakens and kicks me, hard. I stand at attention and walk toward the mirror. The wooden frame of hands moved, twisted, shifting. The glass within the frame is shimmering and shivering. It is like a cloud has come inside the nursery and is passing in and through the glass. I step closer. I raise my hand and place my palm against the surface.

*MIRROR YOU REFLECT ME

WITH REDUNDANCY.

A poem I read in high school invades my thoughts. It pops into my head as my hand breaks through the surface and disappears inside the glass.

Further on, still bridging the gap. There it is. Another hand pressing upon mine. Darryl's hand. Darryl's hand?

Yes. Confirmed when the cloud in the mirror clears. We touch each other palm to palm.

Frightened, I step back and pull my hand back too. The baby kicks and I touch my palm against it. The cloud moves back in while I comfort the baby and Darryl disappears.

I want to smash it.

I want to be in it.

Had I imagined the entire thing? Was I insane?

I am insane.

"Cath. Come back. Please."

I caress our baby with one hand and then a hand passes over, onto our side and holds my hand. It is Darryl's hand. He is here, comforting our baby. Somehow. Some way. My love.

"Darryl."

His other hand, the one with his wedding ring, passes through the mirror onto our side. We fall into him, into his embrace, into the mirror.

"Oh Cath."

His hands make me shiver as he runs them across the baby. The baby turns toward him, and we are halfway in and halfway out.

"He is beautiful," Darryl says. "Like his mom."

"We don't know if he's a he or a she," I say, looking into his blue eyes.

"He's a he, definitely," Darryl says. "He's strong and healthy."

In response to his father's voice the baby kicks and rolls.

"Stand still," I say as I wedge myself further into the mirror. The baby is most of the way through, but I am not through the glass. I can always pull back if I need to. I am not sure why I feel worried. After all, it is Darryl. How I have missed him. Still, part of me remains anchored on the other side.

"Darryl, this is your son. Son, this is your Daddy," I say as the tears stream down my cheeks like waterfalls. Not little petite woman tears, but big fat luscious rainy rain tears. I sob.

Darryl kisses me on the lips. He tastes of autumn, but warm and cool at the same time. Then he bends down, kisses our baby.

"Son, you need to look after your mom for me okay I'm so proud of you and what you will be one day. I love you. I love you both."

I push us, inch us a bit more forward. I consider going all the way through, but something, a feeling holds me back. I want to be there. I want to go through and be with Darryl wherever he is. I want the three of us to be together, forever. Determined, I try to push and push. I want us to get all the way through.

"Don't," Darryl pleads. "Don't even try. We have now. Let's enjoy it while we can. It is unforgiving."

"I want you. I want us, the three of us to be together. Always."

"We only have what it will give us," Darryl says. "Time is a fickle friend or foe. We never know what will come and what will go."

"You're a poet and I didn't even know it," I say with a giggle.

A strong breeze blows through and Darryl steps back. Away.

"Go now," he urges.

"No! Where are you going Darryl?" I cry. "Come back. Please don't leave me. Don't leave us again."

"I'll try to come back, to see you again as soon as I can. If I can. Go now. Somehow. Remember me always. I will treasure you always. Believe in me and then it might let us try to meet once again."

The wind blows in a huge cloud. It blinds us from seeing Darryl. The cloud was white and puffy before, but now it is black and full of anger.

I pull us back.

As I do, my knees buckle.

I drop to the floor and sob.

It feels like I have lost Darryl all over again.

This time though, I am crying for two. Grieving for two.

***

"Cath, are you okay?"

I wake up and remember, but it is only my mom. She is trying to lift me off the floor, but I'm too heavy.

"I called an ambulance," she says as I try to pull myself up and cannot.

"I want to go to bed," I say fighting back another cry fest.

The ambulance arrives, and they came running up the stairs. They test my vitals and the baby's vitals, and once they confirm we were fine, they help me into bed.

Mom is hovering and to make her feel better I say, "He's fine, and I'm fine."

She stops in her tracks. "I didn't realize you asked to know the sex of the baby yet."

"Uh, I didn't," I say, "It is a feeling I have, that he is a he."

The lie seems to do the trick. I feign being more tired than I actually am. The baby seems to be asleep too. After she kisses me on the forehead, mom goes out and shuts the door behind her.

I lay awake for hours, thinking about Darryl and wondering when we can see each other, touch each other again.

***

Every day after our visit with Darryl, I want to go back.

I write exactly what occurs. Keeping a record makes sense. It is the only way I can ensure that my pregnancy brain will keep my memories intact. Writing it all down, obsessing over it, has allowed us to live the same day over and over again. It is like our own version of the Groundhog Day movie, only this time I'm Bill Murray.

Darryl had said it was 'unforgiving.' Did he mean time?

I ask Moni what she thinks. She thinks it rather strange too.

We begin to work together, to research supernatural occurrences. Our target is for events related to travel within mirrors on-line.

We find intriguing articles about parallel universes. Some refer to mirrors as entry points. The research speaks of things like virtual realities and dimensional splits. It also discusses dimensional doorways and the occult. Other than fictional novels though, we cannot find any real proof, although we do find a few claims.

We find a few lists of things you should never do with mirrors like:

Never look into a mirror by candlelight, it may show you a very haunted version of your home.

If you stare into a mirror between two tall, white candles, you might see the spirit of a loved one who has passed away. Their soul can be stuck in your mirror.

That one made my heart jump out of my mouth.

Was Darryl's soul stuck there? It did not seem like a bad or scary place, but he had mentioned the unforgiving thing.

I shiver and go on to the next point.

Always cover a haunted mirror during a thunderstorm. Lightning will release the ghosts.

I tell Moni when I first came into the room, the mirror was partly covered. I hug myself and shiver again.

"First of all," Moni says, "You mom more than likely put it there to keep it off the floor. It is nothing. A coincidence." She looks at me. "Are you sure you want to go on with this?"

I nod and read the next one.

It is a bad omen to receive a mirror from a deceased person's home as a present.

"Oh my God!" I scream and push my fist into my mouth. I do not want to scare the baby, but the mirror has been in our family after a death for centuries. Not as a present with a bow on it, but as a gift and a family heirloom.

I am not sure who had the mirror before it came into our family. I need to find out more about it.

I explain this to Moni who shivers a little herself before she reads the next one.

If someone sees their reflection in a mirror in a room where someone has recently died, they will die soon.

"Whew, we're okay on at one," she says and then looks at me to confirm, which I do with a nod.

I read the next one.

If a ghost wanders your home during the night, a mirror can capture it.

That is creepy. Neither of us says anything about it.

The baby moves.

I scroll on through the article. There is scientific evidence. It mentions quantum mirrors and multiverse mirrors as gateways to other worlds.

"We need to know more. I need to know more about this mirror and how it came to my family. Where did it start? Who gave it to us and when?" I say with a tremor.

"How are we going to do that?" Moni asks, and we both sit contemplating it, alone but together, for quite some time.

The days and the weeks flow forward. Moni and I continue searching whenever we have time.

We track the concept of travelling through mirrors. It goes all the way back to ancient civilizations.

We examine our mirror from top to toe, hoping to find a manufacturer's mark. No such luck.

With the baby due in a week–give or take a few days either way–Moni and I sit together in my kitchen. I can tell by the way she keeps starting and stopping that she has something important on her mind.

"You might think it is a little bit crazy."

"Tell me," I say.

The baby kicks. I caress his foot.

"I'm warning you," Moni says. "It's out there."

"Go on."

"Ok, here goes. Online, I found a woman who is a psychic and a medium. She has an exceptionally good, even excellent reputation. She brings results for the cases she chooses to get involved in."

I lean in closer.

"Aunt Maria does card readings as a hobby. She read up on the woman I am speaking about. She found only good things about her."

"A psychic eh?" I say. I do not understand medium mumbo jumbo. Although I know about that guy who was on television, John somebody. Edwards. I say his name out loud.

"Yes," Moni says.

"You mean the psychic lady will contact Darryl?"

Moni nods.

"But I was able to contact him by myself. I don't know what she could do to help, as we've already been there on our own."

"We should try it. We need her. Not for Darryl, but for the mirror," Moni says. "If it is a travelling mirror. You say it is because you have travelled in it. We need to know more about it. She would be able to test it. Psychics do tests, I mean."

"Oh," I say, and I am more interested now than I had been before. I lean in a little bit closer.

"I explained a little to her about what happened without going into too many details. Her name is Anna August, and she definitely wants to meet you and to see the room and the mirror. I would like to be here too, for moral support. That is, if you want me to be."

"You have to be here with me," I say and the baby kicks to register his vote. I go over to the water cooler and pour myself a glass of cool liquid. "How much does she ask for a visit?" I say after a few sips.

"Five hundred."

I sit down and press the cool glass against my forehead.

"I know it is a lot to ask for," Moni continues, "and I'd like to offer it as a gift."

"That is sweet of you," I say. "But if you and I went fifty-fifty on it, half being a gift from you, then that would be wonderful. How does she collect it? I mean, in advance?"

Moni explains how it would work. We need to send a ten percent deposit immediately as a sign of good faith. Anna would send us a receipt, arrange a date, and time to make a visit in person. On a date agreed upon, the remaining balance would be due upon arrival.

"Upon arrival?" I say. It seems a bit cheeky to ask for money upfront like that, but then again, who knew the protocol for psychics?

Moni gets herself a glass of orange juice from the refrigerator and takes a long drink. "According to their website, delivery is upon entering the home of their client, which would be you."

"Oh, so she doesn't promise anything in return then?"

"Uh, no," Moni confirms. "But I get the feeling this is the norm in the psychic world. When she agrees to take on your case, she fully commits. She wants to ensure that her clients are too. She gets to choose who she wants to help. By telling her new customers she wants a down payment with the balance up front, she'll be able to weed out the kooks."

I laugh, wondering if she would think I was a kook even if I paid in advance. "Is she, is Anna local?"

"No, she's an out of towner, but she knew where you lived. I mean before I told her your address. She said she had been feeling a strange disturbance in this area for the past few months. In fact, it had been so strong that she considered investigating it herself."

This sounds interesting and far-fetched at the same time. "You mean she had a premonition?"

"That's what I wondered too but she said no. Although she often does have them. In this case, she felt a psychic disturbance. Something rushed over her. Made her hair stand on end. That kind of thing."

Watching a scary movie makes that happen to me, but I do not say so. Instead, I agree to send the down payment and to pay her the full amount upon arrival. "We have to find out more, and we don't have a lot of options."

"There are plenty of other options," Moni says, "but Anna has street cred. I'll make it happen as soon as possible."

***

On the third of May, at three p.m., renowned psychic and medium Anna August arrives at my house. Moni and I hide behind the curtains. We watch as she steps out onto my driveway from her vehicle. We are both very curious and want to check her out before we meet her in the flesh.

For the past couple of weeks, we have formed an obsession with Anna. At the same time, I have become obsessed with the mirror since Anna told me to keep away from it. I had not spoken to her, but she insisted Moni pass on the urgent message to me.

The message was, if I went in again, she would know. Our arrangement would be cancelled. Also, that full payment would still be required regardless.

It would be easy money for her if I ignored the warning. She would be paid without having even stepped over my threshold. Her words frightened me enough to lock the nursery door. Just in case.

Anna is around sixty years of age and a handsome woman. She is not pretty; she is handsome. This is not meant as an insult. It is the way she appears to both of us. She is very tall, close to seven feet, and as she wears her hair in a bun on top. It adds to her height even further.

She wears a high-collared, blood red overcoat with black heart shaped buttons. On her feet, thick black wedges. On her face, the slightest touch of mascara, red lippy and nothing more. The dark black hair behind her left ear revealed a black heart-shaped earring. Perfect match to the buttons on her coat.

Anna walks toward the front door with a powerful sense of determination and purpose. She wobbles a little bit on her wedges, and we giggle. When Anna spots us, she winks, and makes a sign of the cross over herself. She hesitates, then makes the sign of the cross over my house.

We have been so distracted and taken by everything Anna has done that we do not notice a man trailing behind her.

He stands close to five feet tall and is black haired and black bearded. He wears a black overcoat, a black cap shields his eyes, black trousers, and shoes. He sweeps along like a dark solitary cloud. We realize the stoop is due to what he is carrying on his back: a small black trunk. Although it is smallish, the weight of it is enough to make him hunch over.

Anna strikes the doorknocker, and we rush forward to meet them.

***

Anna sweeps in like the wind, and the dark cloud blows in not far behind. She extends her hand to me first, taking my other hand. She looks into my eyes and I into hers--which were an odd hue of green with tiny red flecks across the pupil.

"I'm so pleased to meet you at last," she says, reaching out and then stopping before she touches the baby. I nod that it is okay for her to do so, and she places her open hand onto the baby. I expect him to kick to acknowledge her presence, but he does not.

"He must be sleeping," I say. For some strange reason, his not introducing himself with a kick makes me feel like we are rude.

Anna flings back her coat. She turns to Moni and says hello. She introduces us to her husband who is standing in the background stretching his back. His name is Ballard.

I walk over to him, and we shake hands. He needs help getting the chest off his back, so I help him. Afterwards, he stands up straight and tall. He is not so short after all. He is short for a man and Anna in her wedges towers above him.

"Let's attend to the boring details," Ballard suggests.

"Yes," Anna says.

"She means the money," Moni whispers.

I retrieve my handbag from the side table. It contains the full amount, which I hand to Anna, who gives it to Ballard.

"Thank you," Anna says.

Ballard takes the money out and flips through the lot. Assured that the full amount is there, he stuffs it into his coat pocket.

Anna says, "I'd like to see the room now."

The three of us, Moni, Anna, and myself (or four if I include the baby) make our way toward the nursery. I glance back to see Ballard fishing in his pocket for a key which he inserts into the lock and opens the trunk.

I am curious about the key, but more curious about its contents. Ballard continues. I turn my attention back to this business.

"In due time," Anna says as she moves us along. She sees me looking at Ballard with curiosity. She does not, it seems, miss a thing.

Before we reach the nursery, Anna makes a sudden stop. I damn near run into her since I am now at the back of the pack with Moni in the lead.

Anna's breathing changes. She pants, and her cheeks become very flushed. She grabs the wall on her right and the other wall on her left with balled fists and stands there stock-still. Her fists burst open like roses blooming. She lays her hands flat and open onto the surface of the walls on either side of her.

Her head flies back and her eyes open wide, looking upon the ceiling. Her entire body begins to shake and convulse like she is having an epileptic fit.

***

Something pumps through her body then. Whatever it is, I see it making its way through her. I look at Moni, whose eyes are almost popping out of her skull. I reach across Anna's shoulder and take Moni's hand in mine. We stand still, not knowing what to do. Anna continues to vibrate and twist.

Ballard is there then, placing something against Anna's upturned forehead. It is silver.

I see it flash in the light, but I cannot make out what it is. First a blur, then a shimmer. Soon Anna's arms and head drop. Then, she is back among us.

"I am sorry my love," Ballard says. "I didn't expect…" He stops and looks at Moni and I who are still standing together, holding hands.

"Nor did I," Anna says as she takes in a deep breath and releases it several times to calm herself down. "That was a powerful something or someone. May I have a glass of port before we continue?"

I begin to say that I do not have any Port in the house. Ballard, who came prepared, removes a flask from inside his jacket. He twists the cap open and hands it to Anna.

Her hands shake as she tries to take a sip. Ballard assists.

Anna wipes her mouth with her hand. I can still see her fingers shaking as she passes back the flask. Ballard offers me a sip. I refuse due to the baby. Moni refuses too, but thanks Ballard for the offer.

Anna breaks the silence. "And now, let us continue."

***

Before we reach the nursery door, it slams shut. The force is so great I think it might break the hinges. I push my way past the entourage, using the girth of my child to clear a path through.

When I am at the door, I reach into my pocket for the key. Once unlocked, I attempt to turn the handle. I say attempt for two reasons.

One, it does not budge, and two, it is red-hot, so much so that I scream when my skin melts into it. It is like the metal handle welds itself to me and my skin sizzles and smells like I am being barbecued.

My searing flesh smells almost bacony as I continue to try to separate myself from the handle. The next few seconds feel like time has suspended, and I focus my mind on the handle itself instead of the pain. In one movement, I detach myself. The handle moves. For a second, I think it is going to turn and open, but it doesn't.

I look to the left where Moni stands, staring, wondering what to do, but doing nothing. I look over at Ballard who is looking at Anna who has her eyes closed and is mouthing words.

I watch and listen to her mumbles, realising she is doing an incantation or a spell. At least, that is what it looked like based on the fictional television shows I had seen with witches in them.

Do psychics perform incantations or spells? I was not sure, but whatever she was planning, I sure hoped it was going to work.

As that thought crosses my mind, the heat of the door handle increased from a nine to a ten and I cry out in pain. Ballard rushes toward me with the vial of brandy in his hand and splashes the contents over my hand. It smokes and spits and smells like an off Christmas pudding.

It works, and my hand dislodges itself from the handle. Ballard leads me away from the door. I stand still while Moni hands Ballard the first aid kit she has retrieved from the bathroom. He wraps my hand in gauze after spraying it with some burn relief liquid. It cools the temperature of my skin. When he wraps the gauze around it, the pain is minimal.

When we return to the corridor, Anna is nowhere, yet the door to the nursery is standing wide open.

This time, Ballard leads the way with Moni and I following not too far behind. Ballard keeps his right arm out in front of him as if he anticipates the arrival of the unseen and unknown. If he had a cross in his hand, it would not be out of place. I have watched way too much television for my own good.

Once he is inside the nursery, Ballard whispers, "Anna." He stands in the doorway, blocking Moni and I from entering the room.

No reply.

Ballard steps all the way in, still calling for Anna, and we go in behind him.

The window is wide open like it had been on the day when I entered the mirror. This breeze is a violent one though. It blows the curtains forward. They ripple and float above the floor in a ghost-like fashion.

The flying curtains lead my eyes in the direction of the mirror. Moni and Ballard do the same, but this time they are behind me as I walk toward the mirror. The blanket, once draped over the mirror, is now crumpled up in a clump on the floor.

"Anna!" I call out.

Ballard screams his wife's name.

Although I do not know him, the pitch and tone in his voice send goose bumps racing all along my forearms. I turn and look at him, seeing pure fear. It was preposterous to me that he is this freaked out. Ballard is her partner in every single way. Together, their lives focus on helping people connect with their loved ones on the other side. They are pros.

I make my way to the mirror. In one giant step, I walk my entire body into it.

The last thing I hear is Moni screaming my name.

***

On the other side is total darkness.

This is different from before. Scary.

I take two steps forward. Something crunches under my feet. I move a little to the side, hoping whatever it was will not be there, but it is. I move forward, trod on something bigger before I stumble a bit then stop still.

Too scared to move, I realise this place was exactly how I expected the inside of a mirror to look. What I do not expect is the smell. It is dank like rotting autumn leaves and cold. I wrap my arms around myself.

I do not move, hoping my eyes will adjust and become accustomed to the darkness.

Seconds pass. Still, I do not make a step in any direction. I can feel myself rocking on occasion. Standing still with this big of a belly is not an easy task. I feel like I might topple over. I caress my baby bump and try to remain calm.

Where are the forests, the beach, and the mountains? Where are the sun and the autumn breeze? Here, the frozen air stands still.

I wonder if this is a different dimension.

Why does this place feel so unfamiliar when the other seemed homey? I was a fool to enter without knowing that Anna is here.

I hear a crunch and then Anna's voice. "Cath?"

My body shakes as I answer.

"Cath," she says, "you need to get out of here."

I caress my baby bump in an attempt at normality.

"Do you know how many steps you took after you came in?" Anna asks.

I tell her I have not stepped many steps, and yet I had not counted them either.

She asks if I would be able to turn, if I knew in which direction I had come, and I say I think I do.

"Turn yourself around and go in the direction of the outside," Anna instructs. "I'll follow the sounds of your footsteps. The sound will guide me, and we'll get out together."

I think about Darryl when we first met. With these happy thoughts at the forefront of my mind, a memory pushes in. It was about something I had read or watched. About demons in the dark taking on the voices of those we know, sometimes even those we love. In it, the demons pretend to be who they are not.

I quiet my mind and push those thoughts away, gaining strength by thinking of Darryl and the baby. I turn around, reaching my arms out to feel my way. The crunching makes me feel panicky, but I knew I had not gone too far. I walk forward like a blind zombie and feel nothing.

I take two more steps to the left, still moving in the same direction as before, and reach out in front of me again. Still no contact with anything. Two more steps.

There it is. I feel it and step forward. Ballard and Moni pull me the rest of the way through.

Anna grabs the tail of my shirt and comes through too.

We are safe.

We are back.

***

I weep as Moni assists me across the room. I sit in the glider chair as if I carried the weight of the world on my shoulders. I caress my baby bump and hum Frere Jacques to quiet my heart and mind. My baby boy does not respond with a kick, but he is no worse for the wear.

Moni brings a cup of hot tea. My hands shake too much to hold it. She lifts it to my lips, and I have a sip.

In the corner, out of earshot, Anna whispers to Ballard as she takes a pull from the flask. She is shaking and Ballard stares in my direction on occasion and then back at his wife. I had rescued her, brought her back. I wonder what they are talking about, but I am too tired to hone-in-on their conversation.

"How long?" I ask Moni.

"Eight hours."

"It couldn't have been eight hours!"

"It is dark outside. See?" She pulls back the curtains, showing darkness outside in place of the daylight. She leans in and asks, "How was Darryl?"

My son gives me such a big kick that it takes my breath away. I caress his foot through my skin. "Settle down, son."

Moni waits for the baby to settle before she asks, "If Darryl wasn't there, why were you gone so long?"

"I—I don't know," I say, looking in the direction of Anna and hoping she might offer some answers. After all, she is the only expert in the room.

Anna takes another pull from the flask. Once she sees me staring at her, she stumbles her way across the room. "Are you quite alright?"

Anna stands on my left, Moni in front of me and Ballard on my right like I am the centre of a semi-circle. I shiver. Moni throws a blanket over my shoulders.

Anna says, "The mirror has many faces. That one," she points toward it, "ought to destroyed."

"But why?" I ask with chattering teeth. "It has been in my family for decades and it brought Darryl to me."

"I suggest you send it away if you cannot destroy it. It will call you again and tempt you to enter if it is in your house. Next time, you might not be so lucky. Next time, you might be stuck there forever."

"Listen to my wife," Ballard says. "She knows what she is talking about and all she wants to do is prevent you and your child from harm."

"It could have harmed us, but it didn't," I say. "It was dark, and it was dank, but I have been in worse places, far worse places."

Anna hesitates, paces a bit, then says, "The crunching sound. What did you think it was?"

Ballard steps toward his wife, whispering into her ear. They turn toward me again.

"Leaves," I answer. "Dead leaves."

Anna's eyes light up as she looks at her husband. "It was the sound of breaking bones. The bones of others who never made it back."

I gasp and try not to scream. I think about the sound I had heard and wonder if she is making it up, trying to scare me. If I had stepped on bones, what would it have sounded like? Feel like under my feet? They would sound exactly like the ones inside the mirror.

"Now, let's get out of here," Anna says. "We have done all we can. We can be here no more. Mark my words, if you do not destroy that thing, then it is on your head."

As they walk away from me, I call out, "Why didn't you wait for me? Why did you enter the mirror without me? Before, Darryl my husband was there. Everything was safe and good. Why didn't you wait?" I stand up and follow them, expecting an answer, an explanation.

Anna keeps on walking.

Ballard stops, considers saying something. He changes his mind. "Come, my love. This woman does not appreciate your sacrifice or advice."

"Her sacrifice? I went in there and brought her out! I saved her."

"Calm down," Moni says. "It is not good for the baby."

"Get out of my house," I yell.

After Ballard fastens the trunk on his back, he and his wife leave my house.

I stand there with clenched fists as the water trickles down my legs. Dizziness washes over me and I fall to the floor.

***

It is not water after all. It is blood.

I found out only after the ambulance comes screaming up my driveway and the paramedics check me out. My vitals are fine, but they insist we go to the hospital.

Resting, tethered to machines and monitors, I feel grateful my son and I are both doing fine. Nothing more and nothing less.

Moni called my mom who arrives fast. She sat with me, holding my hand, telling me everything was going to be okay. Now, she is sound asleep in a chair.

Looking at her sleeping, I realize mothers are god-like. We rely on them for everything from the moment of our conception. When explain everything is going to be fine, even if we know they cannot know, we still believe them. If they told us the sky was orange, we would have to believe them. Why would they lie to us? Our mothers are nurses, doctors, advisers, or counselors, teachers, philosophers, and our friends. Mothers wear so many hats.

I feel my baby bump, thinking about my own potential to fill the role of mother and sole parent for my son. I hope I can match my mother's strength and courage. If I could get to eighty percent of what she has been for me, then I will be over the moon.

I consider what the doctor has told me. The bleeding was nothing serious. A temporary condition and it had stopped. Baby is fine with a strong heartbeat. Still, the due date is not far away, and they want us to be here.

I drift off, thinking about Anna, disappointed. There had been such a build up to her coming and her offering to help. I had asked Moni to contact her to see if she could fill in some of the gaps. I wanted to know what happened to her before I entered the mirror. What did she know? What had she seen?

I also wanted to know why she had jumped into the mirror before any of us were in the room.

Tears spill down my cheeks in a silent cry. I miss Darryl so. Life would be vastly different if he were here. Life is too short, too precious to waste a single moment.

I fall back against the pillow and close my eyes.

***

My feet lift off the ground. I fly with my monarch butterfly wings out into the open air. I rise up higher and higher into the sky as planes pass me by. Passengers wave out their windows. Birds stop. One sits on my shoulder. It opens and closes its beak in song as if it is trying to have a conversation with me. It flies off, happy to have attempted to communicate with its fellow sky-dweller.

Below me, a small, winged person follows. I caress my baby bump, but find it is no longer there. The winged person below is my child. His wings are blue and black. He is learning to fly. He makes his way toward me, struggling.

"Mother," he calls.

I hover in place waiting for him to catch up.

"Mother," he calls again.

I push myself down until we are side by side. I take his hand.

Together, we rise.

I throw my head back, still holding his hand in mine, and the sky changes from day to night in a split second. The air turns from warm to cold, and the wind picks up and pushes us away.

My son and I cling together, holding fast, flapping our wings in synchronicity. Powerless.

Thunder rolls in. Lightning bolts fling across the sky behind us, below us, getting closer and closer.

A direct hit on my wings. A spark ignites on his.

We plummet back from whence we came.

***

I wake up screaming. So much for not waking up mom.

The dream had been so real, so vivid. It made the monitors flash and beep. The hospital staff came running in and they took control.

"It was just a dream," I say to reassure them. Still, they continue to rush around.

I wipe the sleep out of my eyes.

Something is wrong with mom. They did not come in for me.

They put her onto a hospital bed and roll her out of the room. The wheels squeak her away from me.

"What's happening?" I shout. I try to get myself up, to go with her, to be with her. I have to catch up with the entourage.

I am tethered though. I try to free myself. Not fast enough.

A nurse jabs a needle into my arm.

The last thing I remember is swearing at her.

***

Moni is by my side when I wake. It had been daytime when I fell asleep. Now, it is dark. Everything through the window looks inky black and starless.

As I try to put together the pieces, my son kicks me extremely hard. It is almost like he is reminding me to put him first, as if I need reminding. First, it was that scary dream. Then, mom was in trouble, sick or something.

I snap back to reality.

Moni hands me a glass of water. She and I had been friends for so long it sometimes feels like we had a telepathic connection. Moni is the best friend in the world. I do not know what I would do without her.

"Thank you," I say as I take a sip and feel the cool water making the way down into my very empty stomach. No wonder my baby is kicking like crazy. I need refueling having missed eating today. Not that hospital food is anything to write home about. I ask Moni if she would mind sneaking out and getting me something fast food-ish as a treat.

Being her usual, logical self, Moni suggests I call the nurse. Ask if they could do something for me so as not to interrupt their dietary requirements for myself and baby. It sounds like good advice, although I would have murdered a cheeseburger, fries, and shake.

The nurse is helpful and says she would bring something especially made for me as soon as possible. In hospital language, which meant as soon as I reached the top of the pecking order. First in, first served.

I rub my baby bump with one hand and sip more water to keep the hunger pangs at bay.

"We need to talk," Moni says.

"I'm listening."

"First of all, your mom is doing okay. She had a stroke, but from what I understand, it was not a big one. I don't know specific details because I'm not family, but I get the impression she will make a full recovery."

I breathe in a sigh of relief and remind Moni that she is like the sister I never had.

"I have a sister," Moni says, "but you are my sister of choice."

"Love you," I say.

"Love you too."

We are silent for a moment, and then she says, "I spoke with Anna for you. The visit to your house and into the mirror totally freaked them out. Those two are no novices. She, I mean Anna, has never felt so near to pure evil as she did when she was inside your mirror."

I recall the feeling of bliss when I was with Darryl. The feel of his touch. His connection with his son. What she was saying seemed ridiculous and I say so.

"What do you mean?"

"First of all, I was there too. Yes, it was very dark. It was dank and a bit stinky even, but I did not feel a presence of evil in the air. If evil lurked within that darkness, then it could have taken either of us at any time. We were at its mercy. So why didn't it do anything?"

"She says the devil only wants the souls of the damaged. The ones who have committed evil or done evil deeds. The only exceptions are those who come to him willingly and who are pure of heart."

"And Anna, where does she fit into that scenario? I ask.

"Anna said that if you and the baby in particular hadn't been there, then the thing would have taken her. She says it whispered to her that she was lost, that she was his before you entered the mirror. When you did, a light emanated from the baby. It was not a bright light. It was dim, but it was enough for her to know that you were there. That light led her to you, and at the last possible second, she grabbed you and you pulled her out. Without the baby, without you, she would have been lost, her soul have been eternally stuck in there."

Without thinking about it, I caress the baby's foot. He turns inside me.

I look up as a stranger with a clipboard comes into the room. He wears a frown as big as the Grand Canyon, but is somehow flushed and pale at the same time.

"Are you Cath?" he asks.

***

He is not wearing a white coat, and he is not family or a friend.

I nod, confirming I am me.

In response, he calls out, "Bring it in."

Two delivery people bring in a large, covered item.

Before they unveil it, I already know what it is. The mirror. "What is that doing here? I didn't ask you to bring it."

"Sign here." The man hands Moni a pen. She flat out refuses to sign it at first, but the man raises his voice. He threatens to cause a ruckus, so she signs, but only after, I tell her to.

"We'll figure out what to do with it after these two bozos—no offence—leave."

Moni smirks and so do I.

The delivery people retreat.

"Now what?" Moni asks standing as far away from the mirror as she can without going out the door.

I feel safe where I am on the bed, wrapped up in covers. From here, I can try my best to ignore the elephant in the room. What on earth was it doing here and who sent it?

***

Moni's phone rings, causing both of us to jump. She is busy pushing the mirror to the side near the window.

"I'll be right back," she says.

On the way to greet me, a new attendant sees the mirror and uncovers it. "What a beautiful mirror," he says. "The frame and the wood in particular are absolutely stunning." He runs his fingers over the engraved, joined hands and says, "Japanese isn't it?"

"I—I don't know, but it has been in my family for decades."

The attendant positions the mirror so that it is visible in my peripheral view. Part of it is facing me and part of it faces the window.

He looks at the back of it. "I've seen something like this before. If you ever want to sell it, please call here, and ask for me or leave a message.

My name is Daniel Chung." He hands me his card.

"Uh, thank you," I say as Moni returns to the room.

"Is everything okay?" she asks, looking at the mirror and seeing the attendant fondling it.

"Yes," I answer, "Daniel was telling me he thought the mirror was Japanese. He said he has seen something like this before. Oh, and he would be interested in buying it. That is, if I ever wanted to part with it."

Moni pales.

Daniel checks my pulse. He confirms everything is fine and asks if I need anything.

"What a strange guy," Moni says.

My water breaks.

***

Things happen too fast. The monitors go mad. The contractions begin. I am dilated and ready to push. The baby's heart rate is falling, as was his blood pressure. They wheel me out into the surgery and begin prepping me for an emergency C-section. I so wish Darryl were here with me.

It is all hands-on deck. They drug me up and go in to save my son.

I am out of it, cannot see, or feel anything. I watch hospital staff moving about. I listen to the machines. I hope and pray my son is going to be okay.

They raise him up, so I can see him.

He does not cry.

He is blue.

I scream.

Someone jabs a needle in my arm.

I sleep knowing my son is dead.

***

I wake up and remember.

"Would you like to hold him?" a nurse asks.

I nod.

She leaves the room.

I get out of bed.

My son arrives in a glass case swaddled in a green blanket. He is wearing a matching knitted cap.

She hands him to me. Tears roll down my cheeks as I kiss his cool forehead and see us reflected across the room in the mirror.

I walk toward it.

I'm still a Mom. Holding my son.

I kiss each of his eyelids.

The ground below my feet begins to shake, as the sun screams light into the room and into the mirror and into my son.

His eyelids pop open. He sees me. Knows me.

Then he is gone.

I stumble, holding the lightness of nothing in my arms.

There in the mirror, Darryl is holding our son.

"I love you," Darryl says kissing his forehead.

"I love you too," I say as our son begins to cry.

The mirror begins to spin first slowly, then it picks up momentum. It bumps and grinds, twisting like it is going to fly off.

Hypnotized, I cannot look away.

Darryl's hand reaches out of the mirror, and I take it.

And we're together forever Darryl, our baby and me.

DEATH WISH

IT WAS DIFFICULT FOR him to think of anything else.

He lived in the perfect time. A time when he could find anything online.

Videos and photos. Everything he needed to know about it. Even things which frightened the living daylights out of him! And he could do it at work or at home.

All he had to do was keep multiple tabs open, and when he needed to, switch back and forth. It was like he was a spy, playing a game of cat and mouse which only he knew was being played.

He spent every waking hour—or as much as he possibly could—researching. Arranging and re-arranging pieces of the puzzle. Preparation was the key. Getting it all together, until he was ready. It would be easy then, and with all the facts on the table, he would eliminate the possibility of failure.

"*Failure is not an option,*" he said to himself, wondering who had said it first. Curious, he Googled it. He found a book with the same name attributed to Gene Kranz, Flight Director of NASA's Mission Control.

The problem with researching on the Internet—distractions. So easy to get off track. Down a dark hole. If he didn't watch it, time would fly by and soon he'd be way too old to do it.

And then there were the interruptions. Life had its intrusions, both good and bad. You had to face it—you could go through life doing things you loved or things you hated, but either way, time was getting away from you, and there was nothing you could do to control it.

All one could do was close the door and hope and wish the world away. Sometimes, that wasn't a very good feeling for those people in your life who you loved, like your wife. Or your dog.

Sometimes he felt like he ought to fall to confess everything to his wife. To throw himself at her feet. But then he'd consider how he would feel if his secret wasn't just his secret. How he would have to answer questions, and how his decisions would be open for discussion. Every little bit of him would be pulled apart like a Christmas Cracker.

No, he decided. Secrecy was the only way. Besides, she would worry. And she might involve other people, like his parents or her parents or their friends. Then the cat would be out of the bag.

He wondered where that phrase originated from. He searched it and chuckled at the debate online, especially the German and Dutch 'pig in the poke' comparisons. He scrolled down, wanting to discover the author's name, but gave up when his wife 'he-hemmed,' behind him. He switched the screen to something neutral.

"A few more minutes," he said.

She closed the door behind her.

Whenever she stuck her head inside the door... Even after she was gone... He felt like he was seven years old again and caught with his hand in the cookie jar.

Bloody Catholicism, he thought.

He felt guilty about everything.

It wasn't like he was wanking or anything like that.

He was working.

Mostly, working.

True, he wasn't getting paid, but it was still work. It had a purpose. He searched the word "work." One definition was, 'a form of torture.'

He laughed.

He tried to focus, but he couldn't because he felt so damned guilty. Like his wife was constantly on him. Berating him—which she wasn't doing. His mind cried out, "Don't I matter?" He covered his ears and cringed. The mere thought of her denouncing him, her words cutting through him like butter, made him bite his thumb...

"Do you bite your thumb at us, sir?" he asked the empty room.

"Did you say something?" his wife asked through the closed door.

"No," he said. Then under his breath, "I do not bite my thumb at you."

These were the only lines from Shakespeare he remembered. Like Shakespeare, he was a bit of a drama queen.

He went back to work, feeling guilty now for lying to Jayne.

It wasn't like he was looking at porn or anything like that, either. Some of his mates had their guilty online pleasures, but that wasn't his thing. When they bragged about their conquests, it made him want to disappear. One of his married friends had signed up to several of those online dating sites. They'd send him photos on their phones, and he hadn't even met them in person. And then there were the online porn addicts. They talked about it, even bragged about it.

It made him feel sick. It made him feel ashamed to be a man.

Then again, many of the wives were out buying frilly pink handcuffs after reading that sexy book on the top seller list. His wife tried to read it, too, but being an English teacher, she couldn't get past the bad writing. His wife's friends kept telling her to give it a go. They told her to ignore the writing style, but the teacher in her wouldn't allow her to.

Once again, he was letting his mind stray. He searched the title of the sexy book and discovered an inappropriate puppet on YouTube reading a few chapters. He popped his earphones in and listened and laughed in spite of himself. Someone had gone to a lot of trouble putting it together.

But it was nothing more than a distraction. He needed get back to the task at hand. He hated himself when he couldn't focus, and yet, he was so easily distracted.

Just then, his dog, Buddy barked, and he looked at his watch. Buddy had been outside for nearly thirty minutes.

Feeling guilty, he jumped up and took a few steps toward the door without changing the screen. Buddy barked again, and he returned to close his laptop. Better safe than sorry, he thought to himself as he left the room and walked down the corridor.

"Too little, too late," Jayne said in a laughing tone in his direction, as Buddy came bouncing toward him.

"Sorry," he said, "I only just heard him."

"No worries," she said, "I was closer." Then she returned to reading and marking her students' papers.

He and Buddy made their way back along the hallway and into his office. "Sorry, Bud," he said as the dog sat down on the floor and began to lick his face. "Did you miss me, Buddy?" he asked repeatedly as Buddy barked out a yes.

"I better get back to work, Bud," he said resignedly.

He returned to his office. Sat down, determined now to focus.

He leaned in closer to the screen, all the while weighing the pros and the cons. He didn't write anything down or make any notes. If he did, then someone could find them and read them. Then he'd have to explain everything, and that would not be a conversation he wanted to be a part of, now or ever.

"Want a cup of tea?" Jayne called from the kitchen.

"No thanks," he said.

Distractions and more distractions. Five simple words like, 'Want a cup of tea,' could send his brain spiralling. He'd start thinking about this and that and how everything was connected. Next thing he knew, he'd be a little boy, swinging on the swings in his parents' backyard. Then he'd see himself swinging from a tree in the park. He'd be too exhausted to do any research. Not physically exhausted, you understand, but mentally.

However, today was mostly his day. It was Sunday, and Jayne would spend most of the day marking papers and then preparing dinner. Sure, she expected him to come out of his 'cave' at some point. That's what she called his office. A direct reference to that book she'd seen on Oprah. His wife as a gift had given him a copy, hoping it would bring him out of his man cave. He couldn't remember the occasion, but from what he had tried to read, it seemed like rubbish.

Jayne knocked again.

He had just enough time to click the page over to his company site again before she put her arms around his neck and kissed him on the top of his head.

He hunched his shoulders involuntarily. Hiding his work, imagining that she was interested in whatever he had on the screen.

She had been interested, because she commented on Facebook being open in another window. He felt like such a dweeb wasting time on a Sunday afternoon looking at Facebook. Or to put it another way, he felt like a dweeb for Jayne to think that on a Sunday afternoon he would prefer to be spending his time perusing Facebook – instead of spending time with her. That was not the case at all, and he wanted her to be reassured of that.

But at the same time, he thought that maybe whatever she thought at this point it was a moot point.

He casually scrolled down his work email, pretending to be extremely busy when a Status Update window popped up. He closed it quickly, wishing Jayne would go away.

"Will you be ready to go pretty soon, love?" Jayne asked.

"Sure, give me five minutes," he said, and as she neared the door, "or maybe ten?"

"Ok, ten it is, but you really need to get some fresh air today. As do I. Plus, I'll get Buddy's lead ready, and he can come along, too."

"Good idea," he said, knowing full well Buddy was looking forward to going out more than he was.

***

Suffice it to say that their venture out of doors did not last very long. It led to the mall. Crowds. Wage earners. Time wasters. Next week's haemorrhoid H-ers. He smiled but didn't feel the need to share his joke with Jayne.

Jayne offered to put everything away, so he let her.

He wanted and needed to get inside of his den and close the door. He made like a turtle once inside with his shirt surrounding his head. He sat there like that, seeking solace and silence until he was calm enough to begin his research once again.

When his head popped back up, he could hear Jayne fixing dinner. She was humming along with the oldies radio channel. He imagined Jayne at the stove with Buddy sitting in there, waiting patiently for a taste or two to come his way.

That was the Bud-meister for you. He always waited, and with those doe-eyes watching, you had to toss him something. He was so going to miss that dog.

He cracked his knuckles a couple of times like a professional pianist. Then, he traced his fingers over the keyboard. Google search. What popped up, though, was totally different from anything he had ever seen before!

It was online. There were actual videos of people doing it. Doing it! Watching the first one, he felt almost like he had been the person in the video. His heart was racing, and so was his pulse. He could not believe that just seeing a video could cause such a reaction.

Someone ought to complain about this, he thought and then, I should complain about this. But he wasn't going to. He watched another one, and another, and another. Each time, he felt he was the person of interest himself. Each time, his heart nearly jumped out of his chest.

He turned it off. It was too much. Way, way too much!

He continued playing what he had seen over and over in his head. He couldn't escape it. And the more he thought about it, the more scared he became. The more freaked out he became, the more his courage waned, until he wondered if he could go through with it.

It was all in the eyes. The panic-stricken eyes of the victims!

He considered their facial expressions. Decided that they looked that way because they, unlike him, hadn't done any research beforehand.

He figured that they must've just made up their minds and went for it. This idea he could not fathom.

It was far too risky, and what if they changed their minds?

What if he changed his mind, at the last minute?

He did not want that to happen to him.

He was certainly different from them.

Maybe he was overcautious.

Maybe he was too dull and too boring to be able to change his life—to be able to take control of his life. All due to the fact, that he'd been at the mercy of the Corporate treadmill for so very long. Him and all the other hamsters. On and off, off and on without anything to show for it.

He hated his life. Yes, he loved Jayne, and he loved Buddy—but life is more than just work and bed.

Yes, making love was nice, and cuddling was nice. Friends and family and all that emotional mumbo jumbo were nice. But life had to have more to offer. It just had to! And he was going to reach out and grab for that ring before it was too late.

Because he knew that if he didn't do something to make his existence on this planet mean something soon—then he might as well not have even been here.

He closed his laptop, put his head down, and fell asleep.

***

In his dream, he had no legs. He was just a head and torso, sitting at the desk, typing. He didn't have a special chair, either. In the dream, he was sitting on the same chair as always, with rollers on the legs. When he typed, the vibration of his fingers moving across the keyboard made his torso shift and sway. Since the chair had no arms, his torso would incline in the direction of the hand he was typing with. It was strange, but he wasn't afraid of falling sideways. He felt fearless, and oddly enough, inspired.

Then a song began to play very loudly, somewhere in the background. It was Mozart or Beethoven or one of those classical composers. Something in his head made him yearn to tap his toe— but he had no toes. He woke himself up and let out a scream.

Jayne and Buddy came running, throwing open the door. "You have an Apple imprint on your cheek," Jayne said once she realized he was just fine.

"Sorry," he said.

"Dinner's nearly ready," she informed him.

"Okay," he said.

She made the motion to close the door behind her, but he said it was okay to leave it open. She had a quizzical expression on her face but didn't say anything more.

Once he joined her in the kitchen, he went to the fridge for a beer. They ate dinner in a pleasant but not talkative environment. They loved each other, but sometimes love was not enough.

Not enough when Jayne found out she could not have the family she wanted. She had been through test after test, and everything seemed to be working fine. And then he was tested, and their hopes and dreams just fell apart. He didn't have enough healthy swimmers. That's when any hope of having a family had died.

At first, she was gracious about it. It was almost like she was relieved, because the problem was his instead of hers, which was fine—but it somehow made him feel lesser than a man. He never talked to her about it. Or anyone else, for that matter.

After the initial shock, they considered other options like adoptions, IVF, or surrogates. None of those options appealed to him. In his heart of hearts, he felt Jayne deserved someone better than him. Someone who could give her everything she wanted.

It was about that time when he and Jayne had been driving home from somewhere and they noticed a pet shelter. Homeless dogs and cats. The couple hadn't considered the option of adopting a pet before.

"We could take a look," Jayne suggested.

"I guess it couldn't hurt," he'd agreed.

Once inside the shelter, the barking and meowing hit them hard. Two Cockatoos joined in the chatter.

He felt claustrophobic, and he wanted to get out.

Jayne began talking to one of the Cockatoos, and they seemed to like the tone of her voice. She looked at him with a hopeful expression.

"I don't agree with the caging of birds," he said.

"Hmmm," she said as she moved along toward the cats. "So many of them," Jayne observed. "It would be difficult to choose."

"I'd prefer a dog," he said.

"Hmmm," she repeated.

Consequently, their wandering around the shelter led them to Buddy. His name then was not Buddy.

The shelter staff had named him Buster, and he had been at the shelter for just over a month. He was a big ball of fur, with feet too large for his body. He clumsily padded his way toward them. Stumbling and crashing. While the dog walker tried unsuccessfully to rein him in. But it was like Buster had a one-track mind.

He made his way straight for them. He splayed his body on the ground at their feet. The dog looked right into his eyes, and there was no question that Buster was going to be adopted that day.

"Can I change his name to Buddy?" he asked.

"I don't know—try it on," the dog walker suggested.

"Come here, Buddy," he said. "Come here, boy."

Buddy's ears went back, and he jumped up into his arms. They became a family of three on that day, and from that moment forward their lives revolved around Buddy.

His eyes still welled up every time he remembered that moment. He would miss Buddy, and he would miss Jayne, but they would get over it. They would move on, in time, and they would be better for it.

Or at least that is what he kept telling himself.

In the evening, they went to bed at the same time. She read a book, and he tried to read, but nothing could hold his attention. So, he just thought and stared and thought and stared. And when Jayne talked to him about the book she was reading, he nodded, but he wasn't really listening. She wasn't really expecting him to. Buddy was at the end of the bed, snoring long before they were.

When she fell asleep, he would get up and pace. He didn't let Buddy walk with him, because his paws padding up and down the hallway would have wakened Jayne. At some point during the night, he decided he was acting rashly. He'd told himself he simply had to get through another week at work and then everything would work itself out.

He was stalling, this he knew, but nothing had changed.

It was inevitable.

***

Still, Monday morning came, and the alarm went off.

He walked Buddy and ate some buttered toast. Drank a cup of coffee, and kissed Jayne goodbye before driving to the office. He sat in gridlocked traffic for twenty minutes. He listened to the news and the chatter until he longed for silence. He breathed in deeply as the cars inched forward every few moments.

"Why do I wait in traffic every single day to get to a job that I hate?" he asked himself out loud.

"Why am I such a whinger?" he answered with another question.

Because you need to do something, a voice inside his head said. You need to jumpstart your heart. You need to be fearless. You need to pee or get off the pot!

Easier said than done, he thought. Easier said than done.

In the office, he greeted the receptionist who said the boss was waiting inside.

"Did we have a meeting scheduled?" he asked as he scrolled through the timetable on his phone.

"No," she confirmed.

He felt a drop of perspiration forming on his forehead as he entered his office. His boss stood up, and they exchanged greetings and shook hands like it was the first time they'd ever met.

Odd, he thought, since I've been working here for seven years.

"Sit down," his boss said. It sounded like a direct order, so he did, even though he was in his own office. On his own turf.

"What can I do for you, Sir?" he asked.

"It's been brought to my attention that you have been spending quite a bit of time—no, I have to be straight with you—quite a lot of time lately on Google. You haven't been bringing in any new customers. Quite frankly, I'm—we're, as a firm you know, we're worried, because you're not holding your own. Pulling your load. "

He hesitated for a few seconds. His mouth had come open, but then he closed it, saying nothing.

"What do you have to say for yourself?" his boss asked, "Any, uh, explanation?"

"I—no," he stammered. "I just—"

"Spit it out, lad," the boss-man said. "There must be some kind of explanation!"

He just shook his head.

"Perhaps you are having family troubles?"

"No."

"Alcohol? Drugs? Death in the family? Divorce?"

He shook his head no. If only it were true!

"Come on, man," his boss said, growing exasperated. "Give me something to work with, here. Anything!"

"I-I've been under a lot of stress. A lot of pressure."

"Yes, there you have it now, boy. I know I caught you off guard by coming into your office unexpectedly, but now you're getting the hang of it, my boy. Tell me more. How can we help you? I mean, myself and the partners."

"I don't really know," he said. "I think it might be best if you, uh, fired me."

"Now, now, who said anything about firing you? We haven't come to that point yet. You have seven—count them— seven good years under your belt here. Well, let's be realistic—it's probably more like six and a half—but you're a valued member of our team. We want to help, if you'll let us. How can we help, my boy?"

"If you won't consider firing me, would you consider a leave of absence? Perhaps a month off? Without pay is fine. I don't mind. I—"

"Without pay, you say. Well, there is no need for going without pay. I'll put together the paperwork today. We'll call it, Stress Leave. One month fully paid. Take your wife and uh, Buddy and go on a nice holiday somewhere. Relax." He stood up, leaned across the desk, and they shook hands again.

"Thank you, sir," he said. "Thank you. Really."

"Heather will give you the papers to sign before the day is out. Work today, finish up anything you can and then delegate the rest to someone else. I'll send out a company-wide memo, saying that you're having a month off—but we won't say why, of course." He touched his nose, as if to affirm their shared secret. "That'll be between you and me."

He stood up and walked his boss to the door. His boss patted him on the back.

"You take care of yourself and don't worry about things here. We'll hold the fort until you get back."

"Thanks again, Sir," he said, and he even managed to smile for a moment.

Then he sat down at his computer and returned to his research once again. At the end of the day, everyone gathered around him. He hoped that they hadn't bought him presents or anything. They hadn't.

It was a good send-off. He packed all his personal bits and pieces into his bag, and he felt very relieved when he got back into his car.

As usual, he arrived home before Jayne. He took Buddy for a quick walk around the block and then returned to his computer. He looked at his will and considered making a few alterations.

Jayne was still the sole benefactor. He decided to leave something to the pet shelter where they found Buddy. It was a good sum—they could help lots of stray pets with the money, and in doing so, his life would have meant something.

"Come here, Bud," he said. "You have to look after Jayne now, ok? I'm counting on you."

Buddy jumped up and put his paws on his shoulders. They hugged. He wiped a tear from his eyes.

Together they went to the kitchen. He filled up Buddy's food bowl and then ran some cool water from the tap and filled his water bowl.

Buddy moved straight to the food, but he caught him for another hug. He fought back a sob as he went into the bedroom and began to pack an overnight bag. He threw in just the basics, left his passport on the top of his desk, and then sat down to write Jayne a note.

It read:

Dearest Jayne, I love you more than anything, but I think you would be better off without me. Please take care of Buddy for me. Sorry it must be this way, but I made a vow to keep you happy, and this is the only way.

XOXO infinity.

Your loving husband.

As he drove along the Princess Highway, he thought about the things he regretted the most. He hadn't followed his dreams. He hadn't let Jayne pursue hers. In the early days, they had been a force to be reckoned with. But now, they—well, things were different. She had wanted to travel, to fly, to take off and share adventures together, but he had always wimped out.

He regretted the fear. He loathed himself for the fear.

It made him feel like less of a man. And then, when he didn't have enough swimmers—well, that was the straw that broke the camel's back.

He began to question everything then. Why he had been placed on the earth? What was his purpose?

How he could make things different?

He remembered back to this morning, when he had kissed Jayne for the very last time. Of course, she didn't know it, but he did. Even if they hadn't given him a month off, he wasn't going back tomorrow for anything. No, he had other plans. Other places to be. Other things to do.

For once, in a very long time, he had a purpose.

He had to stop the car then, to pull over. He barely made it out of the vehicle in time. His hands shook as he vomited.

Nerves. Fear. Anger. Humiliation. It all churned through his system, unsettling him.

As he climbed back into the Lexus, his phone began to ring. It was Jayne. He clicked the button to make it stop ringing and sent the call straight to voicemail. He watched as the phone lit up moments later with a message. He pushed the button to listen.

"I just got home and found your note—I don't understand. Buddy and I don't understand." On cue, Buddy barked. "Come home, okay? Come home, and we can talk about this. Talk it over." She sniffled. "Are you there? Are you listening? Listen!" Jayne's voice went quiet for a few seconds. The message timed out. She called back again. "I know you are bloody well listening, you, you—I love you. Answer me!"

He hung up, turned off his phone, and put it into the glove compartment. They would find it there— after.

As he pulled away from the curb, he made the wheels of his car squeal. He revved up the engine, pushed his foot to the floor, and sped away.

He drove most of the night. He felt a bit paranoid that Jayne might get the police involved, but nothing happened. He hoped she wouldn't be too mad at him.

There was no turning back.

Besides, he didn't want to.

After all, he had accomplished everything he wanted—everything he could.

***

Standing at the top of the mountain, his knees shook uncontrollably. He pushed a few rocks off the edge and watched as they tumbled on their way toward the bottom. He listened as they made their way down, clicking and crashing against the stone. Finally, he heard just the faintest splash, and then at last, there was silence.

It was an awesome view—The Blue Mountains—and now, everything he had read about it made perfect sense. When you stood all the way up here, you felt small in size and stature, but a part of something bigger than yourself. You felt at one with the universe, and somehow, unafraid.

Just then, a group of noisy cockatoos made their presence known to him. Their loud, high-pitched screeches made him cover his ears.

You don't have to do this, he told himself. You don't have anything to prove to anyone. You could turn around and go back home to Jayne and Buddy, and no one would be any wiser. Jayne would understand if you simply explained what had happened at the office. She would totally understand and be supportive.

He considered this for another moment, as he watched the clouds pushing their way across the sky.

The truth was, he couldn't live with himself. With the constant fear. It was too much for him to put aside and go back home, pretending that it never happened. If he gave up now and returned to life the way it was, then he wouldn't be able to look at himself in the mirror. He wouldn't be a man anymore, not really. He would be nothing. His life would mean nothing.

"It's now or never," he said.

And when the moment came, he did not think about it any longer.

He was fully committed, for the first time in his life.

He moved closer to the edge, and simply let his body fall forward, starting with his head. It was easy, because of the steep decline. Soon, his shoulders and torso and legs were all sailing downward in perfect synchronicity.

He screamed. He couldn't help himself. He clenched his eyes firmly shut, concentrating as the wind tossed and jarred him like a puppet.

He forced himself to open his eyes, and it was like he was flying.

It felt like he was weightless, and it seemed that he was meant to be just like this—to soar. He laughed as he sank toward the bottom like a stone.

It was all over in a few minutes.

"Totally bitchin'!" he exclaimed as he hung upside down on the end of a bungee cord.

"Again! Again!" he cried as they reeled him back in.

GOODBYE

"**T**ELL ME THE STORY of the first time you met Daddy," my seven-year-old daughter asked even though she'd heard the same story many, many times.

"Are you sure, darling?" I asked, knowing full well what she'd answer.

"Please!" she said, looking at me with those big blue eyes she'd inherited from her daddy.

"The long or condensed version?" I inquired, pushing a fringe of hair out of her eyes.

"Long!" she said, applauding like she'd never go to sleep.

"Shh," I said. "Hmm, now where did it all start?"

"'Goodbye,' Daddy said," my daughter cooed.

"That's right darling," I replied, leaving out the part about her daddy pushing me against the car door.

I grabbed my handbag, put my arm through the strap, and throwing my weight against the door like I was a linebacker pushed it open. Decamping with my right high heeled shoe first, it didn't take long before I realized we'd stopped next to an ankle-deep puddle. Before my brain could register this to avoid my left foot stepping into it, it already had. Still, I was getting out, getting away no matter what damage it did to my favourite shoes.

"Oh," I said, now fully out of the vehicle with my back to the driver.

"Then you stepped into a puddle!" my daughter squealed.

"Yes, and your daddy sniggered as he pulled away with a swerve of the back tire causing the puddle contents to spray onto the rest of me. I brushed the dirty cold stinky water away, flicking it off before it settled on my dress. With the other hand, I raised my middle finger in the direction of the deserting vehicle,"

I stopped myself having forgotten to edit out that bit.

"Why'd you?" my daughter began.

"Never mind," I continued, "just in time to catch a glimpse of my handbag bouncing alongside the vehicle. Ack! That black handbag had given me ten years of happiness because it went with everything and every situation. Dual purpose, it could go either over the shoulder or over the shoulder and across my chest. It had compartments built in for everything including my phone."

"Oh no, your phone!" she exclaimed.

"Yes," I said smiling. "How was I ever going to get myself out of this jam? More importantly, you're wondering how I got to this point in the first place. And I'll get to that in a minute but first I have to assess my situation. Take stock and take control. First, I drained the water out of my shoes as I stepped off the road, through the dewy grass and onto the sidewalk. I put my shoes back on, wet as they were choosing the wet over any creepy night crawlers which might be lurking about and made my way to the nearest streetlight.

"Now, placing my hands on my hips in a Wonder Woman stance, I got down to the business of making a plan to get myself out of the jam I'd gotten myself into."

"It was a nice neighbourhood," she said.

"With lawns tended to and not a weed nor vehicle in sight – they were all tucked safely away in their double or triple garages. Nice houses, contain nice people. Right? So, I decided without delay to choose a house, knock on the front door, and ask for help. I choose the house, lucky number seven and made my way toward it. On the way,"

"You felt sorry for yourself Mommy."

"I sure did. I didn't deserve to be stranded in the middle of unfamiliar territory, late at night, all wet, stinky, and penniless. As I neared the chosen one, number seven, a whir filled the air, followed by the whoosh of an automatic sprinkler wielding its way. I didn't run at first, I was already wet, but as the water stream turned on me, screaming I made a run for it. Now my face was wet with tears I hadn't cried as I crossed onto the lawn of the home I hoped would save me. Number seven."

"You should never talk to strangers, Mommy," my daughter said.

"That's right darling, but I was in trouble and wet and without my phone. You always have your phone and the numbers of daddy and grandma, and Aunt Lil are in it."

"And I know your number, daddy's and grandma's in my head."

"That's right baby. So, back to the story. Aren't you getting even a little tired yet?"

"No, I'm still waiting for the bestest part!"

I continued, "Now that I was here, I wondered what time it was. And I wondered if anyone was home. And I wondered if they were home if they'd help me. I was wet, filthy, and I had no identification. My confidence was dwindling by the moment, as I turned, leaning against the doorbell which resonated from top to bottom of the house, as lights flickered on and off. And I ran. Back toward where I'd been dropped off. Familiar territory as it were. I'd walk to a corner store where they would have a phone they'd let me use and I could call for help and send them the money for the call. Yes, that's what I intended to do until a car rolled up alongside of me and inside I recognized a friendly face. I was really and truly rescued!"

"It was Aunt Lil!" my daughter cooed and of course, she was right.

***

"Riding along in the car with Lil, I recalled my unrequited love interest in Jasper Winters. I'd watched him from afar, his blond wavy hair, blue eyes, his nose with a freckles peppered across it. He was so sweet, so thoughtful. He was always going steady with one girl or another and my friends told my that my obsession with him was getting closer to the stalker stage. Which is why I agreed to go against the one thing I'd always refused to do – go out with a total stranger on a blind date. Yes, it was with the same guy who was now holding my handbag hostage. His name: Adam Trent."

"My Daddy!" she cooed. "That's the bestest part."

I smiled.

"It had been our first meeting, earlier today in the food court at the mall. The meet up place was agreed upon, and it was in a public place. Somewhere we could chat with plenty of movement around us. This setting would take off the pressure. Make the gaps when neither of us had anything to see feel less gappy. Is gappy even a word? I don't know, but you get the gist. Through our mutual friend we agreed it was an opportunity for us to get to know each other face to face. If there was a connection, we agreed in advance to setup the next meeting which would include either a movie or dinner. Next step only if we both felt the connection. Otherwise, we both agreed it was hasta la vista baby! Adios and good riddance! If only I'd known, then what I knew now! Then I wouldn't be in this position. But as the saying goes, hindsight is 20/20. When I first set eyes on his across from the food court he wasn't the kind of guy who would stand out in a crowd. I immediately liked that about him, that he blended in like me and when I rolled his name, Adam Trent on my tongue as I said it, it suited him, and I immediately relaxed."

"Love at first sight," my daughter exclaimed.

"It was," I said. "After we made the introductions, nudged elbows since we were both wearing our mandatory masks he asked what I wanted to drink and off he went to get the coffee. He got my order right, cream and one sugar which showed me he was a good listener I felt hopeful. As we sat and sipped our coffees, we chatted with a sense of familiarity like more than acquaintances, closer to friends. He laughed, not too loud. I hated people who laughed really loud, drawing attention to themselves. Adam wasn't like that. He was considerate, kind, understanding and talking with him felt normal. Or should I say like the new normal since we were chatting freely while wearing our protective masks. Still, I don't think I would have been wrong in thinking, if anyone were observing us, it would be clear to them that we felt comfortable in each other's company. We advanced in our conversation from one thing to the next quite easily and soon he told me that he would be attending University in the fall. I rather clumsily informed him that I was taking a year off. I didn't tell him the specifics, that I needed to earn money before I could return. That was too much information and not something he needed to know about me. Nor did I tell him that I'd won a scholarship, to pursue Classic English Literature."

"I hope to major in Twentieth Century Literature," he revealed.

"Wow!" I exclaimed, "I want to major in Classic English Lit.!"

"With this major love of literature in common, we'd easily make a connection, right? We'd have a bridge from one land of literature to another. He'd discover my favourite authors and I'd discover his and we'd live happily ever after. That's what a part of me was thinking. With the other, I was listening as he sang the praises of his god-like favourite in the world author - Kurt Vonnegut. He continued to commend and extol everything about his choice for the greatest novel of all time - Slaughterhouse Five."

"Until he went too far," my daughter chided.

"Yes, way too far. In fact, so far out of the limb that I had no choice but to defend the true masters, such as Shakespeare, Dickens and Twain, whose bodies of work withstood the test of time. After his face resumed its normal colour, he slung a few Vonnegut-isms into the conversation, such as, "Only in books do we learn what's really going on.""

"It was a battle of the books!" my daughter said.

"Yes, and our first argument. I said, "Talk about stating the obvious!" before firing back with Mark Twain's, "It is better to keep your mouth closed and let people think you are a fool than to open it and remove all doubt." I'd read somewhere that Twain was one of Vonnegut's favourite authors. That was one good thing about him anyway.

"He stood, reached across the table, and kissed me long and hard mask to mask. Right there in the middle of the food court. This was in response to me, grabbing his hand when he said that Vonnegut was the Shakespeare of our time. He'd said it with such conviction, from his heart and his soul that he'd almost made me believe that it was true."

"Them you kissed! Yuck!" she said, covering her face.

"The kiss, although abrupt and unexpected had been hot even though we had masks between us. We hadn't noticed others in the food court staring at us – we let it go on for too long. After we came apart, we set down again and burst into laughter. We immediately decided to see a movie in the mall. On the way to the cinema, that connection waned. If we liked the same movies, we could rekindle it? Then all wouldn't be lost? We chatted about the movies he liked and agreed Tom Cruise's latest would suit both of us – but it had already started so that was a no go. We couldn't agree on any other movie.

"Let's just get something to eat," he suggested.

"By then, it was nearly ten – I was starving too. All we'd had was coffee and that was ages ago, and we'd been smelling the popcorn wafting for quite some time."

"Fine with me," I said.

"In the mall, or out?" he asked.

"I said we should get some fresh air, and so out of the mall we went into the multi-level parking garage. We wandered about for over thirty minutes before he told me that he couldn't remember where he'd parked.

"Then you took your shoes off."

"Vonnegut said, 'We are what we pretend to be, so we must be careful about what we pretend to be.'" He paused. "Uh, you're not very ladylike, are you?"

"'Are you a man?" I asked, quoting Lady Macbeth. Immediately I felt bad about that particular quote and promptly changed the subject, "What about the card? You know, where you pay? Doesn't it say which level you parked on?"

"I know I parked on THIS level," he said, "continuing pushing the button on his key ring and listening for a response like a bird calling for its mate. When the car and the key chain finally found each other, it was close to 11 p.m.

"Now in the vehicle, with ladders running up both of my legs and black bottoms of my feet, I took a deep breath and tried to relax. Food would definitely help with my mood and hopefully his too. It wasn't too late for us to start again. We'd been getting along so well up until the literary clash. Seatbelts fastened, he pushed his foot to the floor and off we went, around the parking lot, and out into the street. We drove around for quite some time, listening to country music. He sang along, while I fought back the urge to say, yippie ki-yay!"

"So, what kind of food do you like?" "he asked after we'd listened to the latest taco joint suggestion on the radio."

"I'm not hungry anymore," I replied, thinking he, given the timeliness of the suggestion wanted to take me to a taco joint. I hated tacos. How could eating a taco, with meat and stuff falling everywhere even fit in with his lady-like criteria? I didn't want to know. Mostly out of spite I said, "Shakespeare is King of Literature and Vonnegut is a mere Jester in comparison."

"Then Daddy slammed on the brakes."

"We were the only vehicle out in the burbs – in the middle of nowhere and that's the story about how your Daddy and I first met," I said, standing and tucking my daughter in. She stretched, yawned, and moments later was sleeping soundly. I closed the door on the way out and went to our room.

ONLY TWENTY

W HEN AUNT GIN DIED only twenty guests outside our family bubble were asked to attend the funeral. This number was limited due to the pandemic. Social distancing and masks were mandatory throughout the day. This included the service at the funeral home, the interment, and the repast.

Since Aunt Gin knew she was nearing the end of her life, she personally selected the twenty guests before she left this crazy world.

As was family tradition she still wanted an open casket. With a new request though. She wanted to be wearing a mask too. Aunt Gin always did have a strange sense of humour.

"How in the Sam Hell am I supposed to deliver an appropriate eulogy? One my sister deserves…when I'm wearing one of those stupid masks!?" asked Gin's younger brother Marvin.

Sitting opposite to Marvin was his second Cousin Frank. He puffed on his cigarette, deep in thought before responding.

"They'll have a microphone, and it'll suffice."

Aunt Gin's favourite niece Mary who was in the kitchen preparing tea shouted.

"It'll be adjustable, the mike, I mean to your height. So, you can make sure your mouth," she wiped her hands on her apron and tired of shouting entered the living room. She stopped mid-sentence now realizing she'd forgotten to bring the tea, she quickly retreated. Returning with an overloaded tray which rattled with every step.

Frank and Marvin were still staring in her direction with their mouths open wide waiting for her to complete her sentence.

"Is positioned right in front of it," she said like no time had passed between her first and her last. Now that she'd said it, she realized that the sheer weight of the tray was making her arms shake. She stooped over and carefully lowered it onto the glass table. "Thanks for the, uh, assistance," she added with a tone which was sharp with sarcasm as she squatted down to prepare to pour.

Marvin and Frank didn't lift a finger. Which was normal for the two of them. A woman did womanly things, and a man did manly things.

She filled the pot, then opened the new packet of chocolate biscuits she'd been saving for company. She and Aunt Gin always kept a box of their favourite biscuits in the cupboard – but they never touched them. Both knew they'd consume the lot between them if opened – so they only came out when company did.

The young woman and Aunt Gin had always been mischievous and in cahoots. Remembering her Aunt being a stickler for presentation, she splayed the biscuits across the plate. She wondered if Aunt Gin was watching from on high. She sighed, even now feeling like a part of herself was missing.

Marvin wasn't fully engaged. Instead, he was staring out the window contemplating having to wear a mask. Frank was puffing away on a new cigarette he'd lit immediately after the other one burned out.

Marvin, finally taking notice of his niece's masterpiece asked, "What on earth are you doing down there?"

"Why, I'm preparing the tea and biscuits," Mary said, stirring the pot, then closing the lid and giving it a swish to hurry it on up.

"Then grab a chair, or something. Don't be squatting there like a…"

"Squatter," Frank said, laughing at his joke since no one else did.

"Never mind, it's ready now," Mary said. She filled the empty cups with the golden steamy liquid. Then added a spray of milk and the usually requested amounts of sugar. She herself took no sugar. "Would you like a chocolate biscuit? They were Aunt Gin's favourites."

"It'd be a damn shame to mess up your swirly design," Marvin said, reaching out and doing exactly that.

"Not for me," Frank said. "Biscuits and cigarettes don't go."

Mary served Marvin his cup of tea first, as he was the eldest. Then she placed Frank's cup on a coaster beside his chair since was otherwise occupied. I.e., lighting up another cigarette. She cringed as he put the butt of the old one onto Aunt Gin's finest saucer.

"Thank you," both cooed.

Mary refixed the biscuit design, glanced upwards. Then gently removed one from each end and crossed the room trying not to spill her overfilled teacup as she walked toward the two-seater sofa. She'd avoided sitting there now that Aunt Gin wasn't sitting beside her. A part of her felt like the balance of the universe was off without Gin in it.

Before Aunt Gin's days were numbered, she and Mary had their dinner most nights on trays in front of the television sitting in the two-seater sofa watching Coronation Street. Mary had been recording the program since then, waiting for Gin's spirit to reach wherever it was going so they could watch the program together like they always did.

That was before Uncle Marvin and Cousin Frank moved in. Before the pandemic made long distance, relatives need somewhere else to live. Now they formed their own social bubble, i.e., they didn't need to wear masks in each other's vicinity. But in a few hours' time, they'd need to don the dreaded masks for the funeral service – no one wanted to be the infector or the infectee.

"What I'd like to know, is why Gin will be wearing a mask. That's first off," Marvin said. "Secondly, why she invited the relatives she did. Why, some of them haven't been in touch with her, or any of us for over twenty years. God knows

Gin tried to keep the family together, through times when sticking together should have been a given."

"Masks are mandatory for everyone, and Gin wanted to be all inclusive. And yes, Aunt Gin was always the one who thought the best of everyone," Mary said.

"Even when it wasn't warranted," Frank said, lighting up another cigarette then adding, "This saucer is getting rather full."

Mary put her cup of tea on the table, grabbed the saucer, dumped it into the bin in the kitchen. She found a chipped saucer in the back of the cupboard – Aunt Gin didn't allow smoking in the house so had no ashtrays – and placed it on the table beside Frank's teacup and saucer. He nodded.

"Would either of you like a refill since I'm up?" she asked.

Marvin held out his empty cup too. "And another one of those biscuits would suit me fine."

Mary grabbed two biscuits, one from each end of the design and placed them on the saucer with a teaspoon, before pouring in the tea, sugar, and milk. "I thank you," Marvin said, blowing on the tea before taking a sip.

Frank declined more tea with a wave of his hand. "None of us contacted those deadbeats because we couldn't stand'em. Nor could Gin – or so I thought anyway."

Marvin dipped a biscuit into the tea and it crumbled and broke. He used the teaspoon to retrieve it, sucking in the soggy biscuit before it dissolved into nothing.

"These biscuits aren't recommended for dunking," Mary said, smiling.

"Now she tells me," Marvin said.

"Would you like me to get another cup and saucer for you?"

"No, you stay where you're at. You've been running around attending to us like you're our hired staff. I'll make do, but thank you for asking."

Mary smiled and bit into her biscuit. She savored it as the chocolate melted on her tongue.

The trio sat quietly, fiddling with their teacups, biscuits, and cigarettes until Mary broke the silence.

"Aunt Gin was feeling remorseful, for losing touch with people. It weighed heavily on her heart and even though the twenty guests – even when she contacted them – did not return her calls or letters, she never wrote them off. In fact, she prayed for them every night before she fell asleep."

Her brother was fascinated and confused. "Gin, prayed for Great Uncle Dave, who practically killed her when she stayed with them as a kid during summer holidays? That's a massive thing for her to forgive. Guess she got soft in her old age."

Mary stood with her hands on her hips, "Auntie Gin was many things, but one thing she wasn't was soft. She'd have kicked their butts if they'd shown up at the door unannounced before she got sick – you know she hated when folks showed up without an invite – but she wanted to mend fences, to forgive and forget." Her words got caught in her throat, and so did the last biscuit she'd just downed.

Frank stood, crossed the room, and slapped her hard on the back. Out flew a partially eaten cookie across the room, landing in Marvin's cup of tea with a splosh.

"Don't you know you're supposed to chew before you swallow?" Marvin said, returning his tea to the tray with a look of disgust.

"I'm so sorry," Mary said, gathering everything up and taking it into the kitchen.

***

Mary rinsed out the cups and put everything into the dishwasher, then went upstairs to use the facilities and to tidy up her face. She'd been crying and didn't want anyone to know. On the way down the stairs, she heard raised voices. She quickly made her way down.

"I loved my sister more than anyone else in the world!" Marvin said. "But I don't see why her asking me to do the eulogy, should be a problem for you!"

"Now, now," Mary said.

"I'd just have been better at it," Frank said. "I've been asked before and I'd be less emotional, less judgmental."

"Why you!" Marvin said, raising his closed fists into the air and waving them about like he was doing an impersonation of a boxer from days gone by.

Frank crossed the room, also with raised fists. It was like a geriatric caucasian version of Ali vs. Foreman.

The two stood toe to toe, eye to eye until Mary started wailing Aunt Gin's favourite tune, "Hush little baby, don't say a world, papa's going to buy you a mockingbird."

Marvin's eyes filled with tears, and he dropped his fists and then lowered himself into a chair.

Frank stood frozen, mouthing the words to the rest of the song while Mary crooned them. When she was finished singing, he walked across the room, to where a photo of Aunt Gin in a frame smiled out at him. He too burst into tears.

"There, there now," Mary said. "It's nearly time to go and here we are arguing."

"She's right," Frank said. "Besides, we'll need a united front when those good-for-nothing buzzards turn up."

"That's if they don't infect us – we're in the midst of a pandemic don't they know?"

"The caterers will take that into account. While we're at the funeral home and cemetery, they'll be setting everything up here to comply with the social distancing guidelines to keep everyone safe."

"But those ignoramuses will still need to remove their masks to scarf down the food and swill down the liquor - and we'll need plenty of the latter."

"For shame," Mary replied. "That has all been managed and paid for by Aunt Gin." Disgusted and having had enough of them, she retreated to her room to get dressed in the black outfit she'd chosen. The men were already in their black suits and ready to go.

"I expect they'll use plastic knives, forks, and paper plates," Frank said. "And they'll have bottles of hand sanitizer throughout the house and garden. Our relatives will need to come inside to use the facilities, but most of the proceedings will be held outside in the garden."

"Pity Gin got rid of the outside facilities," Marvin said.

Mary called down from upstairs, "I forgot to say, they will paint marks on the grass and/or put signage up where people should stand. And as to the facilities, well we've hired one of those portable toilets. Since there's only twenty of them and three of us, there should be plenty of space for all and the lineups shouldn't be that long."

"You've really thought this out!" Marvin shouted. "The three of us can sneak back in and use the indoor facilities on the q.t."

Mary appeared at the top of the stairs, ready to go. "Thank you. I've had plenty of time on my hands to think about it and I wanted everything to be exactly right for Auntie Gin. She and I spoke of everything, down to the last detail. She wanted to remove the burden of me, trying to do it all alone while I was grieving her loss."

Marvin caressed the hairs on his chin. "If it weren't for this damned pandemic, she would have wanted more. She'd have asked for a regular barn burning – or a wake – to celebrate her life. That's what she deserves!"

Frank said, "That she will have – and we'll give her the best one ever – after this pandemic is over. We'll invite the other relatives – the ones we like – and maybe even a few local celebrities. Everyone loved Gin. We'll send her out in the fashion she deserves! But for now, we have to make the best of the situation."

Mary walked across the room, considered sitting – but her dress would get wrinkled, so she returned to the kitchen to fold paper napkins. She'd offered to do as many as she could before the caterers arrived, knowing she'd need something to keep her busy. She thought about everything Aunt Gin had requested to happen on the day. She wanted a toast to be given to her by Marvin, after everyone to partake in some food. She'd even written out what dishes she wanted to be served and chosen the caterer to prepare them. Yes, Aunt Gin had thought of everything. Raised voices in the living room drew her back there.

"Gin said I'd get the lion's share of the business, that's why she made me the executor of her will," Marvin said.

"She said I could keep the house," Mary said. "It's my home too – I've lived here with Aunt Gin for most of my life."

"No one is disputing that fact," Frank said. "You've given up everything, to be here and help Gin when no one else was able to. Why, you could have gotten married, had a few kids…but you chose family over yourself. It's the least she could do, to leave you the house."

Marvin nodded. For once the two of them agreed about something.

"I told Gin I didn't want or need anything from her," Frank said.

"Let's hope she ignored you then," Marvin said with a laugh and seeing that the two were finally in good spirits,

Mary returned to the kitchen to finish up with the folding before they had to leave to the funeral home.

Although the napkins were made of paper, they were delicate and soft. The sky blue with a pink line on the left-hand corner had been Aunt Gin's choice too. As Mary continued folding, it became automatic, so she looked out on the garden and let her fingers do the work.

Her eyes wandered toward the newly planted flowers under the giant oak tree. The baby's breath and roses were finishing up now, but their colours were still vibrant, and they moved around like old friends dancing when the wind wafted.

As she folded the final napkin, her right hand brushed her belly. She did that now and again, although she hadn't been with child for years. The longing never went away. Aunt Gin never told a single soul. Mary hadn't either – not even the father.

And there, buried under those flowers, in the shade of that massive oak, was her child's eternal resting place. Her baby girl hadn't survived more than a few minutes in this world.

Soon, relatives would come, and they'd all gather in the home which would was now hers - and they'd celebrate Aunt Gin's life.

Then Mary like the others would put on her mask, and she'd self-isolate to that very spot under the tree where she'd never feel alone. In the place where she knew Aunt Gin would be standing by her side, holding Mary's baby girl in her arms.

The trio, Aunt Gin, Mary, and the baby would be silent witnesses, while the rest of the family tore each other apart.

PANDEMIC BOY

"LOOK, HERE HE COMES again – it's Pandemic Boy," the tall and lanky and ten-year-old blond-haired boy shouted.

His friend wasn't so tall, or lanky or blond – he was a red-head who laughed before he put in his own two cents. "Where's your cape, kid? Don't you know that ALL superheroes have capes?"

The kid they'd nicknamed Pandemic Boy was younger than the other two but behind his mask he was fearless.

"Not Spiderman," he replied with a smirk.

Although he was younger and smaller in size and stature, not in inches but in feet, with his hands on his hips – looking more like Superman he asked, "And where are YOUR masks?"

This wasn't the so-called Pandemic Boy's first confrontation in pandemic times. In the past he'd used the Superman crossed armed stance to gain control of the situation. It seemed to work well for children and adults. It also helped to know that he had the law on his side.

"We're not followers," the blond boy said, shielding his eyes from the sun with his left hand, then turning his back on the kid so that he and his friend were now standing face-to-face. He mouthed the words, "Let's take off his mask."

The red-haired boy considered this, pushing the toe of his sneaker into the ground thinking that they already outnumbered Pandemic Boy two-to-one. Plus, he was a little kid – although he did have a big mouth and was kind of asking for it. But he was no bully and he didn't want to be one. He concentrated, making a circle in the dirt in front of him, then patted his jeans pocket. "Mine's right here."

"Prove it," Pandemic Boy demanded.

The blond kid glanced over his shoulder at the smaller boy and turned quickly. With clenched fists he advanced toward the younger boy. Tapping his finger on the masked kid's face, he said, "Who-do-you-think-you-are-anyway-kid?" Each word warranted its own tap on the Pandemic Boy's masked chin, and with the height and mass difference the younger boy had to firmly plant his feet in place.

The red-haired boy, said, "I'll put my mask on."

The so-called Pandemic Boy didn't speak, but nodded in approval while his friend, the blond boy glancing over his shoulder gave him the evil eye.

All three held their ground.

***

On some days time stands still. Like all the birds forgot to fly and all the clocks forgot to tick. This was not one of those days and as time advanced, more children came out from wherever they'd been to see what was going on. They gathered around, chatting, whispering, trying to piece together what must have happened to make the three boys stand still for so long.

"I was looking out of my bedroom window," one boy said, "and saw the little masked kid being threatened by the blond kid who was much taller and older. Then I saw there were two of them and I had to come out, especially when the big kid moved in and poked the little kid on the chest," he said, touching his own mask like an adult would a beard.

"I was running over there," a little girl said, "and saw the whole thing. The boy with the mask was asking for it – approaching these two bigger, older boys. I'm surprised the two didn't beat him." Then she addressed the so-called Pandemic Boy, "Hey kid, why don't you do a runner while you can? Before those two older boys beat the crap out of you?"

The trio in the centre of the crowd remained still, like statues. They were listening to the comments made by the other kids who were forming into a crowd, and they weren't. At this stage nobody knew for sure.

Time moved on and the kids wearing masks took the side of the so-called Pandemic Boy and the kids who didn't have masks on sided with the other two. The crowd of kids shifted, broke up into two so they formed two distinct sides. All were ready to act – that's if and when a fight broke out.

Hours went by and no one moved. Not even when mothers and fathers started calling their children home for supper. Nor when parents, grandparents and siblings started calling the children in for bed. Not even when the sun was replaced by the moon and the stars.

***

Finally, Pandemic Boy said, "I'm going home now." And to the bigger blond boy, the one who was still up in his face he said, "Next time I see you, make sure you bring your mask, okay? This is a pandemic, man, and…"

"Okay, okay," the bigger boy said, stepping back. "And next time I see you, make sure you're wearing a cape." He grinned.

"Any colour preference?" the younger boy asked with a smile.

His friend, the red-haired boy who was now wearing a mask said, "It depends if you're a Batman, or Robin, or Superman fan. Me? I'd wear black."

"Same," the younger kid said.

They all went home.

THE VISITORS

"**W**AIT A MINUTE," SHE said, before opening her front door.

She'd been inside for nearly thirty days – in quarantine. Stepping out, the mere act of stepping outside now, felt risky even though she'd only been quarantining to protect those she loved – and others she didn't even know. She adjusted her mask, took a deep breath, and opened the door.

There was a welcoming committee waiting for her and she felt much like Queen Elizabeth must've felt when she stepped out onto the balcony of Buckingham Palace. Albeit her small but comfortable two-bedroom home did not have the glitz and glamour of a palace. For a second or two, she thought about giving them the royal wave but in the end changed her mind when they began applauding.

Embarrassed, even though a mask was covering most of her face, she looked up to where the sun was high in the sky, and felt the warmth of its rays. It felt good, breathing new, fresh air – even though the mask held her back from inhaling deeply. A song by John Denver began playing in her mind. She hummed along nonchalantly.

The applause had ended without her realizing it. and there she was stood like a pig in a poke while all and sundry waited for her to say or do something. Lots of tear-filled eyes, all peering at her over their own masks. No two masks were alike. She scanned the guests, zeroing in on the eyes whose owners she thought she recognized. In her mind she played a game of Who's Who Under Which Mask.

One person in the crowd there was no doubt about who she was due to her size and stature. It was her granddaughter Emily. Those green eyes, the same as her own stood out as they looked back at her over the purple mask. Emily's favourite colour changed often, but she was pleased to see that it hadn't changed in the past thirty days. She'd grown taller though. Emily waved and said, "Hello Grand-ma-ma."

"Hello, my darling Emily," the woman said, smiling with her lips under the mask and over it with her eyes.

The woman hesitated, then panned the audience from left to right nodding as she acknowledged each of them.

First there was Brandon. He was a big hockey fan, and his mask had a Toronto Maple Leaf on it. "Go Maple Leaf's!" he said. She gave him the thumbs up. At least someone still had hope they'd win the Stanley Cup again.

Next to Brandon, was his wife Emily's mother. Her mask had a I heart Jamie Oliver message on it. She smiled at this, wondering if her interest in Oliver might help her to cook a decent roast beef one day. She caught herself in this bitchy thought and ashamed of herself moved along.

Next was Mr. Bob Moody. He was a neighbour, a grumpy old fart who she had no idea why he'd felt the need to join in wearing a construction worker's mask. He waved, with a familiarity she thought strange, however she waved back to be polite.

Bored now with figuring out who was who, the rest of them turned into a blur as she waited for someone to do something or to let her know what they expected her to do. Should she make a speech? No, that would be daft. It had only been a thirty-day quarantine. She couldn't hug them. Or get any closer than she already was to them.

She had the dreaded feeling someone wanted her to make a speech and wondered how she was meant to give one, one that would be heard and understood through the thick cotton mask. Then she thought about politicians on television, like the Prime Minister. When he had to speak, he always removed his mask, said his piece, and then put it back on again. If it was good enough for the Prime Minister, then it was good enough for her. She removed her right ear from the loop, then moved on to the other side.

The guests gasped, then moved further away. All but her little granddaughter.

"Grandma loves you," the woman said, blowing a kiss in the direction of little Emily.

"I love you, too," Emily replied, as her parents now at her side moved her back.

Satisfied now to have felt the sun, to have been out, to have seen those she loved and had spoken with little Emily, she bowed, stepped back, and closed the door behind her.

The telephone immediately began to ring and ring. She did not answer it.

THE HOUSE

T HE ROOM WAS BARE, except for the vacant built-in bookshelves which flanked the fireplace.

Empty bookshelves always made me feel melancholy. Like the previous owner had taken all their friends and memories along with them but they'd forgotten the structures which had held and displayed them while in the house. Consequently, when I left a house, for whatever reason, I always left one of my books behind (I'd buy two of a favourite book), so I'd hope whoever the new owner was they'd enjoy it as much as I did. To me it was like introducing them to a new friend. If that makes me sound overly sentimental, I don't mind because my dear husband always said that of me.

As I crossed the room, adjusting my mask I noticed something tucked up against the wall as thin as a wafer. It was a small rug.

"What on earth is that there for?" I asked. Even though it was threadbare and small, it would have been better, in front of the fireplace. At least there the pitiful thing would have had a purpose. I often do that, giving inanimate objects feelings. In the literary world that's called personification. I use that device so often, my husband calls it Maggie-fication.

August is the name of my husband. And yes, he was born in the month of August, a Leo, whereas I'm a Capricorn.

As he came up alongside of me, I shivered. I was always feeling the cold.

Speaking through his mask said, "Whew it's hot in here love. Why are you trembling?" He unbuttoned his thick woolly cardigan, a gift from our son Andrew, and removed it. He laid it across my shoulders then moved across the room.

I snuggled into it and uttered, "Thank you," as I followed him.

The agent who was an old family friend, wore a mask reflecting the real estate firm for which she worked. She audibly moved about the house in the other room while we got a feel for the place on our own.

Soon thereafter, she entered the room from the doorway nearest to the object I'd spotted on the floor. We met in front of it, like she'd overheard my question.

Judy Marsh, our agent's name and for over twenty-five years, seemed at a loss for words which was very unlike her. Her and every other real estate agent on the planet.

"Isn't the fireplace magnificent!" she exclaimed.

I turned my body toward the warmth, whereas August, who often accused me of reading too many Agatha Christie novels, among other things, now bored and wanting to get on with it, moved nearer to the doorway.

Judy said, "I heard the question you asked a few moments ago. Full disclosure," she touched her nose. "This house has a bit of a history."

August now interested rejoined us.

"What kind of a history?" I asked.

Judy continued, "No sense telling tales if you don't like it here. In that case, we can just move on to the next house. I have a few more lined up. So, what's the verdict on this one so far?"

August said, "We haven't seen the whole place yet, it's too soon to tell and,"

I finished off his sentence as people who have been married for a long time tend to do, "And it's unkind of you, to let us fall in love with the place – not saying that's the case here – and then lower the boom."

"Lower the boom indeed," August added.

"Spill it!" I demanded, as August took my hand into his.

"Let's go into the kitchen," Judy said. "I'll pop on the kettle and make us a nice cup of tea. I stocked the cupboard with a few things like Earl Grey Tea and biscuits, for such an occasion. Then, all shall be revealed."

August, hearing a cup of tea and a biscuit were on offer, followed Judy into the kitchen and I, as the saying goes, brought up the rear. We walked along a hallway, which had lofty ceilings but was rather dingy since there was no skylight - if we bought the place, a skylight would make this hallway homier.

"A skylight would be an improvement," August suggested, as he and Judy entered the adjoining room through a pair of swinging doors like one would expect to see in an old Marlon Brando western. "These will have to go," August said, as the door swung and hit his behind before I could get there and stop it. He stood there, hands on his hips with his mouth open with no words coming out.

As I pushed through into the room, I could see why August was speechless, because oh, my, what a spectacular view! The kitchen and dining room were adjacent, in a huge open plan rectangular space, with glass windows and doors stretching all the way from one end to the other and looking out upon one of the most magnificent gardens I've ever seen. I so wished it were springtime, so that everything would be in full bloom, but autumn here was beautiful too, with trees flaring up wearing their fall colours.

"Dash would adore this," August said. Dash was our baby boy dachshund.

"He sure would," I said, as Judy, now behind us, played Mom by pouring the hot water into the teapot.

Neither August nor I could take our eyes off the beauteous nature awaiting only a few steps away. "May I open the doors?" I asked.

Judy nodded, and August did the honours. Immediately the sounds from the outside flowed like music into the kitchen. There were cicadas, blue jays, sparrows, cardinals, a tree toad…it was blissfully musical – until a few moments later when a neighbour's lawnmower screamed into action.

"Tea's ready," Judy called.

"Perfect timing," August said, closing the sliding doors and clicking the lock closed. "Hello darkness my old friend," August cooed. It was one of his favourite tunes to sing – a classic from Simon and Garfunkel's repertoire.

"It's not dark in here," I said, as Judy poured and served the tea. To be honest I wasn't a fan of posh teas like Earl Grey. Give me a cup of Typhoo any day. I added two teaspoons full of sugar – double the norm with good old Typhoo and August did the same. As we sipped, rejecting Judy's choice of biscuit – the gingernut – we waited for her to begin telling us the story to which she had alluded.

***

"First of all," Judy began, "No one has lived in this house in decades."

"Decades," I repeated, "How can that be?"

August emptied the remnants of his tea. Judy immediately made a motion to refill his cup which he rudely avoided by putting his hand over the top of it.

Judy smiled. "Not everyone enjoys my favourite brew I guess." She refilled her cup, then continued. "The place has been up for sale over the years. We've hired staging specialists from all over the state, hoping their input would help to sell. Thus far, it hasn't worked."

"Makes no sense," August said. "It sure would be less echo-y if the place was furnished." He lifted his empty cup and sighed.

"Would you prefer a bottle of water?" Judy asked and without waiting for a reply she went to the fridge and pulled out three bottles and set them down in front of us. I had a feeling this was going to be a long story.

A strange sound, coming from the garden struck our ears simultaneously. August pushed back his chair, scanning the garden which was now only partially lit as the sun was setting. "Can you see anything?" I asked.

August had eagle-eye vision, although he was older than me. "Shhh," he said. We waited listening carefully, but the sound wasn't heard again. August returned to his seat and sat down in it with a shrug.

Judy said, "Its best if you keep your comments and questions to yourself until the end. I want to finish before, I mean, as quickly as I can."

August said, "We're old, and getting older every minute. We're bound to forget any questions we might have if this tale your spinning takes much longer."

I patted August's hand. "If you have any questions then type them into your phone." I'd been trying to get him to use the Notes function in his phone for quite some time. I, myself, used it for many things including the grocery list. I'd suggested he use it for the same purpose. Still, he'd come home without what we needed and gone back again – this time with paper in hand.

"Maggie," he said, "You know I don't like to be reliant upon technology."

"Being reliant upon trees," Judy chimed in, "Does not bode well for the future either."

"A piece of paper's battery doesn't die!" he exclaimed.

"But a pen runs out of ink," I said, smirking, then patting him on the hand again, handed him a pen and paper – both which I always kept in my handbag for such occasions.

***

"I'll begin at the beginning," Judy said.

Under the table August shuffled his feet, and I could tell that he was growing increasingly impatient and thinking, "Get on with it, woman!" because that's what I was thinking too.

Finally, Judy got down to the point. "When this location was first settled, three people die here."

She waited, for us to react but neither of us did. We'd already grasped that something terrible had happened – and deduced that it must've involved deaths, murders, and/or mayhem. Even my arthritic bones could feel that something terrible had happened here. I wrapped my arms around myself, feeling chilly again. August did the same, but he was warmer than I since he'd previously reclaimed his cardy.

"Originally, a church was built here in the 18th century. After it was destroyed, and three people died – leaving only the bookshelves and fireplace – all religions swore never to rebuild a house of God here. Thus, cottages, homes, stately home, bungalows, and eventually the design of the two-story California split bungalow in which we're standing now were built to suit the owners needs and requirements for the allotted time in which they lived. And so, many parishioners, churchgoers, and families have made this their place of worship and/or home.

Let's start from the original church. In the mid-18th century, a community began in this location, one of the first established in Ontario, after many immigrants chose this place to settle in and to build their new future.

Two such people were Lady and Lord Charleston, who became quick leaders in the community and who offered up the funds to build the first church without any recognition to themselves other than a small library, in the rectory, in which books could be read and borrowed by the community on the subjects related to religion. To make them comfortable while they studied or read, a fireplace would be built in the centre of two such bookshelves.

Because of the significance of the request, much research was done into which wood, would be the most durable over time. One immigrant from Italy, spoke highly of the Mediterranean Cypress, saying that he witnessed an altar in a Roman church made from this wood that had survived a fire which destroyed the rest of the building. It was decided to send for some trees they could grow locally, and to also order an ample supply be delivered by ship to Canada. As time went, the same man spoke of the supernatural powers this tree from his old country had. Because of its strong aroma, families planted the trees near their loved one in cemeteries across the country, to keep the demons away and to ensure the souls of those they loved made it across to the other side."

A few of the other parishioners were not happy with this blasphemy and suggested they use Canadian trees only for the venture. Lord and Lady Charleston overruled the motion, and the community awaited the delivery of the wood for the rectory and in the meantime built the church and went on to build the school, and other buildings. Newcomers flocked to the community, choosing to settle in a place which provided services allowing all to settle in more quickly.

The wood arrived and the rectory was built, but not without some hardship. First, a man taking the log down from the ship, was crushed when several logs broke loose and crashed down upon him. After that, more precautions were taken, but those who had warned of blasphemy whispered amongst themselves in a knowing fashion.

Years later, and the colony without a name, it was suggested that it be called New Charleston, and so it was named and for many generations, all were served by the community, and the population grew in leaps and bounds. Lord and Lady Charleston died, but their portraits were painted and placed above the fireplace in the library of the rectory between the two bookshelves. Against strong public outcry, the library was called The Lady Charleston Archives since the family donated their collection of books to fill the shelves."

I unscrewed the lid on the bottle of water and took a swig, while August glanced at his watch. The sun was now setting and most of the back garden was in darkness, but for a single spotlight which was provided by the moon.

"It is in this church, where the deaths occurred."

August and I moved closer, hoping she'd get to the point soon. My stomach was growling. For it was way past dinner and beginning to converse with August's in a duet of hunger pangs.

"Gingernut?" Judy asked, waving them in front of us. We politely declined. "Why don't I order a pizza? While it's being baked and delivered, I can continue with my story."

"No pineapple," August said. Pizza with pineapples was a real pet peeve of his. "Pineapple is meant for upside-down cake, not for pizza pie."

"I couldn't agree more," Judy said, pushing speed dial on her phone.

"No anchovies," I said, trying to persuade my grumbling tummy to quieten.

***

"In 1847, a woman, a stranger came into the community in the dead of night looking for her husband and young son. She knocked on doors, causing quite a ruckus since it was after midnight. Community members came out of their houses, vying to help her, and formed a search party using lamps to lead their way. It was that kind of community, who joined to help others, even strangers. No one questioned her motives, story, or sanity.

The month was October, so it was chilly, but before the first snow had fallen. They trudged, searching until the sun rose, then regrouped to eat, drink, and find out more from the woman who had been too exhausted to scale the place with them. When she arrived, she was promptly housed and put to bed after a strong cup of tea with a splodge of whiskey in it to ensure she slept through the night.

After more discussion and confirmation no one had seen head or hair of the husband nor the child, they ate together with food provided by the women's society at the church and discussed what to do next. It wasn't like today, where you could easily print up posters and duct tape them up everywhere., nor was social media an option. Instead, an artist was employed, to sketch the family based upon the mother's description. The woman's name was Reba; her child's name was Jacob, and her husband's name was also Jacob.

One evening, quite late a local saw the woman Reba enter the church, holding the hand of a child. He wondered where the husband was, but giving it no further thought he went to bed.

Reba had taken her son to the church to light a candle on the alar to thank Jesus for bringing her husband and son back to her. The door of the church hadn't been secured because Jacob Senior would be joining them soon. A gust of wind, which was so fierce it blew the flame and caught her sleeve on fire and since she was holding her son at the time, his outfit also caught on fire. Jacob the elder entered, and ran toward them, leaving the door all the way open. More angry wind followed him, as he closed the gap between himself and his loved ones. The church, which was made from local trees went up with them in it in no time at all.

The community hall, where the church women were serving food to the volunteers smelled something burning first, and ran out into the streets. Most of the volunteers were also firefighters, but their resources at the time were limited. They did what they could to save the church, but it was too late for it. The rectory wasn't engulfed yet, so they managed to get the Priest out and to save as I have said the bookshelves and the fireplace. The family of three perished…burned to nothingness. Ashes to ashes as the saying goes."

Judy took in a deep breath, took a sip of water, then the doorbell rang. Telling the story had taken a lot out of her, so, August offered to collect the pizzas, but Judy saying she had to pay – she could put it down as a work-related expense – eventually went to the door. She returned with the hot and delicious smelling pizza pie, and we tucked in without speaking for a while other than the oohs and ahhs as we partook in the tasty feast.

Now content and with full bellies, Judy continued with the tale.

"Since then, it says the ghosts of that family, haunt this house. Whatever people see, scares them so much that they go running out of here screaming. And through the years, houses have been rebuilt on this property through the centuries, but no one has ever lived here for any length of time."

It was getting extremely late; Judy's story had taken quite a while to complete.

"Could you please fast forward and bring us up to the present?" August asked, again more rudely than he or I expected him to. It was past his bedtime and getting testy wasn't entirely his fault.

Judy apologized. "This house was built twenty-five years ago. It's been bought, sold, rented, renovated – you name it and more times than I have fingers and toes to count - no one wants to live here." She glanced around. "Yes, it shows well, but there's just something about it. Something which sends folks running. Especially at this time of night. I wanted to see if it happened to you, too."

"So, we're your friendly guineapigs," August said, abruptly pushing back his chair. "Let's get on with the tour. What's upstairs?"

I didn't move.

"You have no idea; I mean absolutely no idea why people would act in such an extreme way? It makes little to no sense to me. Surely you would see whatever they saw."

"I never see," Judy said.

"Well, that's bizarre," August said.

Judy smiled. "I know. And that's why, let me just say this, that spiritual folk like psychics, mystics, soothsayers, witches, warlocks – you name one and they've been here – yes, they've even exorcised this location from pillar to post and still, the thing that sends everyone running, including all of the above still happens. Each one of them ran for the hills, screaming – and never returned."

"Stuff and nonsense," August said.

But the more she spoke of it, the more frightened I became and the more willing I was to believe it, because as time wore on, I was becoming increasingly more cold. In fact, I was shivering like someone had walked upon my grave – even though of course I wasn't dead. Yet. Just thinking about it made the hair on my arms stand on end.

Judy stood. "Now you know what I know. The price is already low, but is still negotiable. The owner wants it to be sold and out of his hands – yesterday. Why don't you have a look upstairs, get a feel for the top floor?"

August said, "We could buy it love, knock it down and reconstruct something to suit our needs like a bungalow. We'd still be ahead of the game and have ample funds to keep us going for the rest of our lives."

With shaky knees, I also stood holding firmly onto the table. It sounded good, in fact too good to be true.

Judy said, "It is heritage designated. The bookcases and the fireplace must remain intact. This is not negotiable. In fact, I cannot accept your offer unless you are willing to put that into writing."

August and I walked out of the kitchen, as if in a trance, ending up standing on the rug which was now in front of the fireplace. The roaring fire spitting and lighting up the room made me wonder why I felt even more cold.

"…electricity," Judy said.

I'd gone off in my mind to book land and missed what she was saying.

"…turned it off. The water too."

I ran my hand along the centre bookshelf, now having the gist of things, as August left the room. I turned and followed him as did Judy. He stopped at the bottom of the staircase, looked to see where we were, then began climbing. I grabbed onto the banister and up I went too. About halfway, the railing felt wobbly, as did my knees. My feet seemed to sink into the wooden stairs, making me feel unsteady. August was already at the top. I noticed he was lighting his way using the flashlight application on his phone. I felt proud he'd finally found use for one of the applications I'd recommended he try.

When I joined him at the top, we looked down at Judy who was waiting with her phone pointed in front of her – also using the flashlight application. "I have to lock up soon," she said.

"We'll just have a good squidge around," I said, as August moved away from me towards the door at the far end of the corridor. As I walked, the thick carpet under my feet seemed squishy, so that hurrying was difficult to do. August threw open the door, displaying a bathroom decked out in peach with a sink, tub, toilet, and shower. The bathroom was adorned with accessories – one of those carpeted rugs thrown around its base. The style wasn't to our taste, and I said so, as we closed the door and moved on to a bedroom, smallish, decorated in blue with cars driving across the walls and stars which lit up when we pointed the flashlight at them on the ceiling.

"I like those star lights," August said, the child in him coming out. I was surprised he didn't like the cars on the wallpaper too. Maybe he did, but of the two he preferred the stars.

"Yes, let's take them down and put them over the fireplace – that's if we buy it," I said.

We moved on to another bedroom, a guest room, full of flowers of all sorts, kinds, and colours. Sunflowers were stenciled onto the back of the door.

"Very homey," I said, as we moved on down the hall to the final room: the master bedroom. It occurred to me that a house this size ought to have more than three bedrooms.

August said, "We can build more rooms on the land, when we make this into a bungalow. So much space is wasted here."

We looked at the en suite which was also very outdated with peach – although there was a spa bath adorned with gold taps and fixtures. And above it, a large bow window offered a panoramic view of what we assumed must be the back garden.

August climbed up upon the bath, taking my hand as he did so. We stood together; side by side looking down upon the garden as three figures appeared. Lined up by height, on the left was a man, although given his stature one might have thought that he was a boy. His attire included a bowed hat, linen shirt with frills above the waist coat, knee-length jacket and breeches proved otherwise. Holding the man's hand was a boy whose jacket fell just below his waist, while his pants ballooned at the knee his dark locks spilled out from under his cap. Completing the three was a woman, holding the child's hand. She wore a thick quilted overcoat which covered her clothes and a sleeping bonnet upon her head – like she'd come out into the night unexpectedly. All three figures' full faces were transfixed by the moon and the stars, either that or they were under a spell.

"Are they for real?" I whispered holding on to August's shoulder, but before I could finish, three pairs of eyes looked directly at us and simultaneously they let out a shriek in such high-pitched voices which must've woken up every dog in the neighbourhood. They three said,

"Every day, we come here to burn."

We covered our ears, as they repeated their siren song then flames, starting at their feet and moving up engulfed them and soon their shrieks turned into moans as they crumbled to the ground into heaps of ashes.

I screamed. And then something happened which hasn't happened in all the years we've been married – August screamed too.

We climbed out of the tub, ran down the stairs, past Judy and out the front door in a speed which two old geezers like us would never have believed to be possible. We got into

Judy's car; she'd driven as she was showing us the property. When she got in, she took off, squealing her tires as she went.

When we'd put ample distance between us and the house, Judy said in a matter-of-fact way, "I'll put together a list of other houses for you to view first thing in the morning. We'll find you the perfect home. There are plenty of beautiful places on the market for you to choose from." She glanced at us in the rearview mirror.

I was still shaking and holding on to August.

"Would you like to tell me, what you saw?" Judy inquired.

"Didn't you h-hear them?" I asked.

Judy shook her head in a no.

"Trust me, you're the lucky one," August said. "Now take us home. We're staying put."

August and I never spoke of the house ever again.

A MURDER

I SAT IN MY car – too afraid to get out.

From behind the tinted glass, I could see it all – so why put myself in jeopardy? Why risk infection when all I wanted was a little bit of nature.

Why not just stay home then, pet? I heard your soft-spoken voice asking me inside my head. Just like you were here, sitting in the passenger seat beside me. You, being my late husband Gerald – forty-two years married before COVID took him out. Yes, my Gerald succumbed to the virus at the very beginning of this crazy time in our lives. Before it was even called a pandemic by those who said they were knowledgeable.

Even when it was confirmed officially that Gerald had been exposed to it and was infected – he didn't believe it. He'd only given in to being assessed because I'd convinced him to come along with me, you know like we said in our vows in sickness and in health. I'd been in the vicinity of someone who'd contracted it while volunteering at the foodbank. I didn't have to get tested, but figured better safe than sorry and I put myself into voluntary fourteen-day quarantine – at least Gerald and I could be together.

When the results came in, Gerald had it and my test was negative. Because we'd been in each other's pockets, odds were I had it too, just was asymptomatic so into quarantine we both went happily together like we'd been for the forty-five years we'd known each other.

We were prepared to face the thing together head on, then I was told to keep away from my Gerald, limit my contact – to keep a door between us, wear a mask, wash my hands often – you know the drill. I took the guest room; Gerald had our room. We said good night to each other through the wall, just like the folks did on the Walton's family.

One night when he couldn't sleep, I serenaded him through the wall a few choruses of the song we'd had our first dance to in high school, a song called Make Me Do Anything You Want by A Foot in Coldwater. I hummed it to myself, as I took in the goings on outside. A group of Canada Geese were eating the grass a few feet away. I rolled the window down a little, so I could hear their chatter. I took a deep breath, allowing the outside air in, but the fresh air didn't stop me from remembering the next part, the hardest part, when Gerald was taken from me and admitted to the hospital. I wasn't allowed in the ambulance with him, and he went downhill so fast I never saw him alive again.

I called the kids first. Of course, they are all grown up now with kids of their own. Kids, goats. Children is of course what

I mean. Not sure when I reverted to the common description. Probably because Gerald isn't here to tell me not to.

Our children couldn't come due to social distancing restrictions. Their areas were back in Stage 2. Besides, the risk of catching the virus themselves, the risk of taking it back to our grandbabies wasn't worth taking. We face timed – with a kind nurse's assistance – but Gerald didn't speak. By this time, the smile had gone from his eyes, and I knew.

After the interment – no one came to the funeral besides me – I didn't know what to do with myself. It was even worse after the insurance paid out. All our lives we'd scrimped and saved – and now, he was gone, there was nowhere to go – not with the pandemic lurking in every corner – and my Gerald wasn't there to share it with me, so there was no point going in the first place. All that money and I couldn't think of a single thing I wanted or needed, besides Gerald.

As autumn approached and the leaves began to fire up, countless times I pointed a particularly stunning tree out to no one. And then there was Thanksgiving on the horizon. Usually we prepared the family feast – with the regular Canadian fare – like Pumpkin Pie, Cranberry Sauce, Turkey, Ham, Stuffing, mashed potatoes, veggies, and coleslaw. Gerald usually carved the bird while I organized everything else. Then we'd go around the table and everyone, even the littlies would say what they were thankful for in the past year. I remembered little Kevin's declaration he was the most thankful for "Bampa," – Grandpa. Gerald's eyes had lit up that day like the sun coming out from beyond a cloud after several days of rain.

My daughter suggested that I "host" a Virtual Thanksgiving Dinner. Her heart was in the right place, but the idea was absurd. On my own I'd do up a Turkey TV Dinner and eat it while watching A Charlie Brown Thanksgiving.

So back to me sitting here in this blasted automobile, with the tinted windows up – too afraid to get out of my car. As my eyes roam over the walkway, I spot Sonny and Evelyn Marshall and before I get the chance to duck – they spot me. They make their way toward me. They heard about Gerald's passing and want to pay their respects and it's too late for me to start up the car and back out of this parking lot.

In front of the car now, wearing masks, Sonny taps on my window while Evelyn goes around to the passenger side.

"Hello," I say through the closed windows. My phone rings. I point to it, letting them know I need to deal with a call, then see who the caller is – it's Evelyn on the line. "Hello, again," I say, as Sonny walks around the front of my car, stopping briefly to look at me through the windshield, before moving on and joining his wife.

Evelyn says, "We heard about Gerald. We are so deeply sorry and just wanted to stop by and tell you so. Also, to say if you need anything, anything at all please call us. We'd like to be there for you as much as we can during this pandemic." Sonny put his arm around his wife.

"I'm okay," I say. "Thank you for the kind offer and for dropping by." I hang up and put down the phone hoping they will go away.

Sonny says something, which normally I would know what as I'm fairly good at reading lips, but with these masks on anyone can say anything. He and Evelyn wave as they return to the path and off they go.

I watch as they join hands, as they become smaller and smaller. When they are gone, a black crow lands on the hood of my car and looks in at me through the tinted glass. I roll the window down and say, "SHOO!"

The crow moves toward me, ruffles his feathers, and replies with a defiant "CAW, CAW!"

I roll the window back up again and watch the thing pacing on the hood of my car. Leaving a trail of bird prints on my dusty vehicle. I start up the engine and spray water up onto the windshield. The bird doesn't budge. I swish the wipers across several times. Still the thing looks at me, shakes his head, then SPLAT it poops. I honk the horn, and watch as it lifts off, hovers, poops a little more, this time hitting the headlight before it takes off toward the water.

A group of crows is called a murder. When Gerald died, from a man-made virus which was unleashed onto our planet, his death was not called a murder – even though it damn well should have been called a murder.

I reach into my handbag and take out the mask. I put one loop through my right ear and the second through my left. I make sure it's sitting correctly, over the nose, under the chin. I step out of my car and into the sunlight.

Good girl, Gerald coos, as a murder of crows form a circle over my head, and I step in front of a moving vehicle.

SANS MASQUE

H E STOOD ON ONE side of the room and she on the other.

Both dressed – or overdressed – is how she perceived his appearance to be. Polished was the first word that came to mind but something about him looked too slick. Like he wanted her to fall more in love with him more than she already was.

At least he'd shown up – even though she'd refused to do what he'd asked her to, and this was their first in person meeting.

They'd met in a dating app. There's no law against that – yet. They'd developed a relationship over time. He always ended his messages with a throbbing heart emoji. She always signed off with a "yours truly," like she was ending a letter. She was a newbie to the dating app. scenario but with the strict pandemic laws in place, how else was she going to meet anyone?

After a little over two months of messaging and emailing, he asked to meet her in person. She reluctantly agreed. In a way, if they never met, she could imagine he was everything he made himself out to be. More importantly, she didn't want to seem too eager or desperate.

He'd gone to so much trouble, arranging everything including the venue he planned to take her to. At first, she couldn't believe her luck. While she waited for him to confirm the details, her emotions went from excited to skeptical. Could he really reserve such an exclusive venue just for the two of them? When he texted the specifics, she'd let out a hoot, then responded with a smiley face emoji. Her first of the relationship.

After that she immediately went to her closet and slid open the mirrored doors. She riffled through the coat hangers, until she found her most expensive dress – the one she called her posh frock. This she so named in memory of her late mother. It was a knock off design number which she'd purchased online and her most proud fashion possession. She held it up against herself, looking in the mirror and trying to decide which jewelry she'd accentuate it with: faux diamonds or pearls? She decided on the former.

On the morning of the big event, she'd woken up early, to check her inbox. She half expected a text or message saying he had to cancel. In truth, a part of her hoped he would cancel, but her mailbox was empty and there'd been no text messages. She'd gone into the kitchen, to make herself a cup of coffee, and then checked again in case he'd been in touch. This time she even looked in the junk file – it too was empty.

Throughout the day she kept herself busy. First by taking a long steamy bath and exfoliating. Followed by a light lunch. Again, she checked for messages and finding none, she went ahead and styled her hair, then did her nails. Before she applied her makeup, she trolled through social media. Finding no evidence of his recent activity, she stepped into her highest pair of high heels – the ones that made her legs look the longest. She finished off the look by applying a layer of candy apple red lipstick and stepped in front of mirror. Perfect.

Except for one thing: her matching clutch bag. She transferred her phone and debit card into it, then went back for her lipstick and now she was ready for anything.

As she stepped out of her front door and applied her mask, the taxi arrived. She'd booked it the night before ensuring she would not be too late or too early. She wanted the timing to be perfect for their first meeting in the flesh.

***

He spent the day double-checking everything, like he always did on such occasions.

He looked forward to finally meeting her in person. Online she seemed shier and naiver than any of the others he'd chatted with. She seemed so timid, so unreal that she'd flat out refused to send him a naked photo of herself. Naked meaning sans masque.

Before she agreed to meet him, he had to reassure her that the guidelines would be followed. Well, not just followed, per say, i.e., she required no less than his personal guarantee that they wouldn't be interrupted.

When the leaders around the world fell, the international government formed to fill the gap. With the I.G. at the helm, the world demanded more severe penalties for non-compliant social distancing hooligans. The newly formed International Pandemic Associates (I.P.A.) were authorized to enforce the social distancing laws using any means necessary.

After the world leaders fell there was a fierce public outcry. Social media was flooded with misinformation. The people demanded justice, taking to the streets with their placards and peace signs. When they couldn't be silenced, and the prisons were filled to the brim public executions were written into law.

Through it all, he'd managed to hang on to his money, and he wasn't afraid to use it when it worked to his advantage. He'd greased a few palms to book the venue and to hire the staff and to ensure that they would remain undisturbed. The eye on the premises observing them – he could do nothing about. S.D. cameras as they were everywhere.

His tuxedo had been collected and was still wrapped in the plastic cover which it wore on the ride home from the dry cleaners. It had been in quarantine in the garage until needed. One could never be too careful. The standard time for quarantining fabrics was forty-eight hours. To err on the side of caution it had been left in the garage for a full week.

When he was fully dressed, the last thing he did was apply his mask before he stepped into his vehicle. There was little traffic and parking was easy.

He wanted everything to be perfect.

Just like he hoped she would be.

***

She stepped out of the taxi onto the pavement and closed the gap between herself and the venue.

On the ground, written in chalk on the sidewalk was a message addressed to her. It read, *Darling, follow me*. She smiled, and followed along the trail of hearts etched on the stones. Every now her fingers sought reassurance from the mask covering her face. It was like another layer of skin now.

Into the open doors she went, following more hearts leading her along the corridor.

At last, she arrived hoping that her true love, her soul mate, was waiting.

***

Across the room their eyes met. She in her black sleeveless dress and he in his black tuxedo.

"You came!" he said in a strong affirmative voice.

"Yes," she replied in a breathless whisper.

She slowed the beat of her heart, by taking in the room. He attention to detail was impeccable. The table was set for two, with the finest of table wares including crystal, and silver. The table stretched the length of the room. In the centre a magnificent candelabra radiated romance.

"Please take a seat," he said.

She sat at her end and he at his. Before an uncomfortable silence could set it, he clapped. Two waiters arrived through a door she hadn't noticed. Dressed from head to toe in full body suits which would not have looked out of place on the moon, they approached. With their gloved hands they filled the champagne flutes, and their bowls with a light consume.

He clicked the side of his glass with a piece of cutlery, and she did the same. At weddings, this ritual once was performed as a request for newlyweds to exchange a kiss. The mere thought of it, unmasking in public made her shudder. In this new pandemic world, the clinking indicated that the initiator wanted to offer a toast.

"To you," he said, raising his glass.

"To us," she said, blushing furiously, hidden under her mask.

The waiters arrived periodically bearing trays. After their final presentation of flambéed Cherries Jubilee, the servers bowed. This indicated they would not return.

"If only I could kiss you," he said, more loudly than he would have liked to but loud enough to account for his mask.

These words from him ignited her. Before she knew what, she was doing, she'd stood up and blown him a kiss. She sat back down again and imagined the kiss floating through the air across the table like a feather.

He caught it, pressed it to his lips. "It's not enough," he cooed.

She launched back her chair again. It scraped through the silence.

Her high heels click-clacked as she crossed the floor. She stumbled with excitement as she made her way along the table toward him.

As she moved toward him, the air conditioning wafted her sweet, sweet perfume in his direction. Until then, he'd only been witness to her coral blue eyes and her small earlobes under which the mask straps were set. His heartbeat so quickly, he was certain it would burst from his chest. To calm himself, he turned his wedding ring around and around on his finger, wondering if this girl was worth it. Was she enough for him to risk breaking the law? Would he die for her?

"Stop!" he shouted, raising his hand violently in the air like an angry school crossing guard.

She still in flight, she bit her lip under the mask.

He secured his mask in place.

As the eye in the wall blinked behind her, he whispered, "Did I forget to mention, that I am married?"

She continued rushing toward him, as the doors behind him swung open.

"Did I forget to mention I'm with the IG?" she inquired, as the two men in space suits tasered him to the ground.

Acknowledgments

Dear readers,

Thank you once again for choosing my book! I hope you discovered a story or two which touched your heart and/or made you smile or laugh.

Thank you also to the wonderful friends, family and the team of people who have supported me and my writing over the years emotionally, as well as those of you (you know who you are) who assisted with technical things like proof reading, editing, et al. I seriously couldn't have done it without ever single one of you.

Thank you all a million times over!

Fondest love,

Cathy

About The Author

Cathy McGough is a Canadian author whose work spans children's literature; young adult fiction; literary fiction; psychological thrillers; poetry; short stories and non-fiction. She lives and writes in Ontario, Canada with her family.

Also By:

FICTION

EVERYONE'S CHILD

RIBBY'S SECRET

PLUS SIZE GODDESS

THREE FRIENDS

PLUS SIZE GODDESS

LITERARY FICTION

INTERVIEWS WITH LEGENDARY WRITERS FROM BEYOND

NON FICTION

103 FUNDRAISING IDEAS FOR PARENT VOLUNTEERS WITH

SCHOOLS AND TEAMS

POETRY

PAINTING WITH WORDS – A POETRY COLLECTION

+

CHILDREN'S AND YOUNG ADULT BOOKS.